"I'd never ████████████
to endanger said."

"A pity you don't extend those sentiments to include yourself," Raoul murmured softly. "Because by coming to my room you have endangered yourself, Claire—or is that what you had in mind? Did reading your lover's letter awaken a longing inside you?"

"No!" Her denial was smothered with the raging heat of his mouth, his tongue compelling her to give him the fervid response his kiss demanded.

"I despise my desire for you," he said raggedly, "but if you tried to leave now I would come after you."

Claire tried telling herself that she would hate herself to the end of her days if she gave in to the feelings exploding through her. But Raoul aroused a blind need in her that would not respond to reason or logic.

Books by Penny Jordan

These books may be available at your local bookseller.

For a list of all titles currently available,
send your name and address to:

Harlequin Reader Service
P.O. Box 52040, Phoenix, AZ 85072-2040
Canadian address: P.O. Box 2800, Postal Station A,
5170 Yonge St., Willowdale, Ont. M2N 5T5

PENNY JORDAN

darker side of desire

Harlequin Books

TORONTO • NEW YORK • LONDON
AMSTERDAM • PARIS • SYDNEY • HAMBURG
STOCKHOLM • ATHENS • TOKYO • MILAN

Harlequin Presents first edition December 1984
ISBN 0-373-10746-3

Original hardcover edition published in 1984
by Mills & Boon Limited

CHAPTER ONE

'Darling, I'm sorry about this, spoiling what was supposed to be your holiday treat too.'

'Being with Uncle Henri is far more important than spending the day shopping with me,' Claire assured her godmother. 'It was just lucky that the hospital managed to get through to you before we'd left the hotel.'

'Umm.' A worried frown creased her godmother's forehead. 'Henri has had these attacks before of course, but . . .'

'You must go to him,' Claire told her firmly. Her godmother's second husband had suffered from angina for several years and Claire knew that her godmother was deliberately playing down her concern because she didn't want to spoil what had been intended as her birthday treat to mark Claire's twenty-second birthday.

'There's a flight back to Paris in just over an hour. I could be on it.'

'You *will* be on it,' Claire corrected. She glanced at her watch, surprised to see that it was still only seven in the morning. The call which had disturbed their sleep and altered their plans seemed to have come hours ago not a mere fifty-odd minutes. 'I'll help you pack and ring down to reception to tell them that we'll be checking out. I'll come to the airport with you.'

'No, Claire.' Susan Dupont spoke firmly. 'No, I

want you to stay on here and enjoy your day as we'd planned. You're looking so tired, darling,' she added softly. 'I wish I could do more to help you. If I could only pay Teddy's school fees for you . . .'

They had been through this discussion so many times before that she knew what her goddaughter's response would be before it came. Although Henri was a good and kind husband, she was solely dependent on him financially, and both she and Claire knew that if she did pay Teddy's school fees it would have to be without the knowledge and permission of her French husband, who, while he allowed her to spoil her goddaughter upon occasions, saw no reason why he should be responsible for that same goddaughter's brother's school fees, and this was something that Claire would not allow her godmother to do.

'Now promise me that you will spend the day shopping and enjoying yourself,' Susan Dupont pleaded. 'The room is paid for for tonight, and I'll speak to reception and have them forward the bill on to me.'

Claire smiled, signalling her acceptance. Two days in London staying at the Dorchester, all expenses met by her godmother, had been a delightful surprise birthday present, and even if she did not really have the spare cash to shop at the more exclusive stores she knew her godmother had visualised for the treat, she wasn't going to add to her distress by refusing to stay on at the Dorchester when her godmother left. She could easily fill in time wandering round the art galleries and museums, it would give her something to write to Teddy about when she next sent him a letter; and if she returned home all she would be doing would be moping about the small flat which was all she could afford at the moment.

Unconsciously she sighed. Life hadn't been easy since the death of her parents. Teddy had only been eight at the time, and because their parents lived and worked abroad, he had already spent two years at the exclusive and expensive private school their father had also attended. Ten years separated brother and sister. Claire had been on the point of starting university when her parents died. Like Teddy, she too had attended boarding school; her parents had been comfortably enough off for her to share in all the 'extras' the school provided, and she had not really given a thought as to how she would spend the rest of her life.

Then her whole world came crashing down around her. In six short months she had grown from a carefree teenager into an adult. Her father's generous salary ceased with his death, and apart from a modest insurance policy there had been no provision made for the future. There wasn't even a house to sell as her father and mother had lived abroad at his company's expense.

The family solicitor had tried to be as gentle as possible. Teddy would have to leave school, the man had told her, there simply wasn't the money ... The proceeds of the insurance policy could be used to buy a modest house and provide a small income. But, rightly or wrongly, Claire had ignored his advice. His school and the friends he had made there were Teddy's whole world. If she took him away from school she would have to pay child-minders to look after him while she was at work and being taken away from his school so soon after losing their parents was bound to have a profound effect upon him, she decided, and so, instead of taking their solicitor's advice, Claire had used some of the money to pay for her own secretarial training, using the rest, carefully eked out over the years, to pay for Teddy's schooling.

Inflation had caused school fees to soar and over the last two years the money she had put aside hadn't been sufficient. A large part of her own salary went towards keeping Teddy at school. Her job was a good one, she worked for the Managing Director of an advanced electronics company based within half-a-day's drive of Teddy's school, but she didn't earn anything like enough to pay for six more years' schooling. Teddy was exceptionally clever, so his school told her, almost definitely Oxbridge material, and for the past few months the problem of how to raise the cash to keep him at school had constantly taxed her mind. She had no real financial assets. Her small Mini was already on its last legs, and the only thing she could think of was to try and get an evening job to supplement her daytime earnings.

This brief stay at the Dorchester was very much an unaccustomed luxury, but she was determined not to add to her godmother's problems by letting her see how disappointed she was that she could not remain with her.

'Now promise me you'll go down and have breakfast. Don't stay up here on your own,' Susan Dupont cautioned when her case was packed. 'Who knows, you might run into that gorgeous man we saw downstairs last night.'

Her godmother was an inveterate matchmaker, and

Claire subdued a small grimace. The gorgeous man her godmother referred to had done nothing for her. Oh, he had been gorgeous right enough—far *too* gorgeous with that thick dark hair, and those unusual green eyes. And despite the formal tailoring of his European suit there had been no mistaking his Middle Eastern origins. They were there in the arrogant pride of his profile; faintly cruel in a way which had sent shivers down her spine and made her think of herself as foolishly imaginative. She had disliked him instinctively. There had been something in the way he looked at her, a careless scrutiny that observed and dismissed with languid hauteur coupled with an unmistakable contempt that burned her pride.

She had seen him again later, in the restaurant, dining with a group of men. Unaware that her gaze had rested on him she had flushed uncomfortably when her godmother followed it and remarked teasingly, 'Mm, there's definitely something about those tall, dark, forceful-looking men, isn't there?'

To cover her embarrassment, Claire had replied acidly, 'He's probably the sort of man who thinks he simply has to dangle a diamond bracelet in front of a woman's eyes and she'll jump right into bed with him.'

Her godmother's rich chuckle had surprised her. 'My dear,' Susan Dupont had responded roguishly. 'I suspect that most women, if they thought such a gorgeous male creature was even thinking about taking them to bed, would be offering *him* the diamonds!' She had laughed again at Claire's shocked expression, noticing the sudden tightening of her lovely full lips with a faint sigh. She was full of admiration for the way Claire had shouldered her burdens since her parents' death, but it sometimes seemed to her that Claire was old before her time, not physically but mentally. There had been no time for fun, for the careless enjoyment of dalliance with the opposite sex, before the blow had fallen and now Claire seemed to concentrate all her energies and time on her job and her younger brother. If only Henri would allow her to help, but he had grandchildren of his own and Teddy was, after all, no relation.

'No, don't come to the airport with me,' Susan Dupont reiterated when Claire followed her out on to the steps in front of the hotel to wait for her luggage to be placed in the waiting taxi. 'Go back inside and have your breakfast.' As she got into the taxi she placed a cheque in Claire's surprised hand. 'This is the rest of your birthday present, darling. I want you to buy yourself something nice ... something ... sexy ...' she added with a twinkle. 'Something that would appeal to our friend from the restaurant last night.'

She was gone before Claire could protest. The cheque was a generous one and Claire already knew that she would not spend it on herself. She would use it to replace those items of Teddy's school uniform which most needed attention. Twelve-year-old boys grew so quickly ... She suppressed a small sigh.

It was all too easy to imagine the sort of 'something' that would appeal to the insufferably arrogant male nature she had sensed lurking below the warm olive skin and cold green eyes of the man her godmother had referred to. Rich silks and satins. Fabrics with a sensual appeal that would bring the glitter of sexual appreciation to those strange eyes. He would like his women supine and obedient, toys to be played with and then discarded when other, and more important matters took his attention. Unknowingly, her mouth hardened, and she was oblivious to the appreciative looks directed towards her by the hotel staff as she stepped back inside the foyer.

Slenderly built with fine bones, she had an air of fragility of which she herself was unaware. Silver-blonde hair which she wore in a shoulder-length bell because it was easy to maintain, framed a classically oval face. Long-lashed grey eyes surveyed the world with a cool aloofness that had been born the day she woke up and suddenly found she was alone with full responsibility for an eight-year-old boy. Always neatly groomed, her clothes were useful rather than alluring. Neat suits and high-necked blouses which she wore for work, bought normally in end-of-season sales. There were no 'pretty' clothes in her wardrobe, apart from the ridiculously expensive gifts she received from her godmother; beautiful silk undies, a cashmere jumper, things she never wore without thinking how much they cost and how that money might have been eked out on more practical garments. Of course she longed for nice clothes, for luxuries, and perhaps when Teddy eventually left university . . . She pulled a brief face. By then she would be in her thirties . . . It was a subject on which she refused to dwell.

There had been several men at work who had approached her for dates, but once they learned about Teddy their interest had waned sharply. And who could blame them? She was certainly not prepared to enter into any relationship which was one of mere sexual indulgence, and yet what man would want to marry her knowing she was responsible for a young brother? That problem was one she refused to dwell on too deeply. Of course she had had the normal feminine dreams. She had envisaged for herself a husband, a family, at some dim date in the future, after she had left university and enjoyed her freedom for a few years, but now she was resigned to the fact that she would probably never marry, and since she was not prepared to go from one affair to another, she had found herself coolly freezing off any male attempts to get closer to her, knowing in advance what would happen when they learned about Teddy.

Thousands of women lived alone these days anyway; she had a good job, a comfortable if small flat. When Teddy was qualified she would be able to travel . . . and yet somehow the picture of her future did not appeal. Although she enjoyed her job she was no career woman. Of course she did not want to batten on to a man simply to escape being alone. She wanted to love and be loved, Claire admitted as she headed for the lift. She wanted to share and enrich her life with another human being.

Her room was on the second floor, where the corridor was carpeted in a richly warm crimson and cream with a luxuriously thick pile. The room she had shared with her godmother was almost as large as her entire flat, and far more luxuriously furnished. Dressing in a soft tweed suit in mauves and lilacs with a toning grey silk blouse, she brushed her hair into its neat bell, applied a discreet touch of make-up and then picked up her bag and key. Over breakfast she would decide how to spend her day.

At first when she stepped into the dining-room she

thought she must have mistaken her directions and that she had inadvertently strayed into a private room. A large party of Arabs—all male—were seated together in deep discussion, and her own entrance occasioned an immediate and embarrassing silence which held her immobile on the threshold of the room until a waiter came forward and led her to a table.

All the way down the length of the room Claire was conscious of male eyes following her progress, studying her, assessing her, but the scrutiny she was most aware of was that which came from ice-cold green eyes that seemed to follow her every step, carelessly dismissing while still assessing her.

It was an unnerving experience, and she was dismayed to discover how much her hands trembled when she eventually sat down. She should have breakfasted in her room, but it was too late—and too obvious—to get up now and walk away.

As her composure returned she realised that she was not, as she had thought, the only female in the room. Several tables away a young Arab girl was trying to feed a small baby, strapped into a highchair. The child, a little boy, was protesting volubly, pushing away the proffered spoon, and Claire could tell that the girl was getting impatient with him. Twice she slapped the small plump legs, raising crimson marks, making the child cry loudly in retaliation. The girl was too uncaring to be the child's mother, and Claire guessed that she must be his nurse, but there seemed to be little sympathy between them, and she was aware, as she glanced up from her own breakfast, that the man with the green eyes was also studying the little boy and his nurse, with a frown.

When the proffered spoon was pushed away for the umpteenth time the girl lost her temper, forcing it into the small mouth. The result was inevitable. The child started to cry loudly, and his efforts to avoid the unwanted food dislodged the dish holding it, spreading it over the table and the floor. The girl threw down the spoon, smacking the chubby legs hard as she pushed away her own chair. Claire noticed that as she stood up she glanced at her watch, hesitated, and then saying something in Arabic to the gathered men, walked towards the door.

The baby was still crying, quite hard now, and against her will Claire felt herself sympathising with him. He had been naughty with his food, but perhaps if the girl had cajoled instead of forced he might have been better behaved. He was wriggling violently in his chair, and Claire gasped as she saw it tilt, rushing instinctively to steady it before it fell.

Close to the baby was enchanting, with soft olive skin and huge tear-drowned dark eyes. He clutched hold of her blouse, the crying stopping as he gazed up at her. He wasn't even secured properly in the chair, and Claire wondered a little at the child's parents, allowing such an inexperienced and uncaring girl to have charge of him. Was one of the men seated at the table the child's father? She glanced towards them and found herself pinned where she stood by the sharply cold glance of the man with the green eyes. What was the matter with him? she thought, unconsciously touching her tongue to suddenly dry lips. Did he think she was going to run off with the baby? His eyes dared her to so much as touch the child, and perhaps it was that, or perhaps it was the piercingly forlorn cry the baby gave as she started to move away that prompted her next action.

Almost automatically she turned back, smiling a little as the baby, sensing victory, lifted his arms. She half expected the man watching them to tear the baby out of her arms, but surprisingly no one moved. When she had been training to be a secretary she had often supplemented her income by baby-sitting and although it had been a couple of years since she had last held such a small child she found herself instinctively slipping back into the mothering role.

The olive cheeks were faintly flushed, his skin hot, and Claire guessed that he was probably teething. His clothes were obviously expensive but crumpled and stained with food. Suddenly realising what she was doing Claire moved to put him back into the chair. He cried protestingly, clinging on to her. Torn between common sense and an inborn instinct to comfort him she glanced across the room. *He* was still watching her and it was something in that look that impelled her towards defiance. Turning away from the chair and walking back to her own table, she soothed the complaining howls, murmuring soft nonsense which seemed to have the desired effect for the cries gradually ceased. She had just reached her table and turned when she saw the men enter the room.

Later she decided she could only have acted by blind instinct, because surely there hadn't been enough time for her to register the menacing appearance of the gun; the silent intent of the man pointing it towards the now empty highchair, and even as he sought her out she was pushing over the sturdy table and crouching behind it, cradling the baby as she heard the sharp splinter of china and another noise that chilled her blood.

Gunfire was something she was familiar with from television, but she had never before experienced it so close at hand. The silence that followed those staccato spurts of sound was, in its way, even more terrifying than what had gone before. Dimly she was aware of running feet, of doors being closed, of someone approaching, a dark hand resting on her shoulder. She knew she tensed, unable to turn and look up, her too-vivid imagination working overtime, so that when she was eventually able to move the first thing she saw was the gun, held casually in the hand of the man standing over her.

Fear thundered through her body, leaving her drenched in perspiration, and trembling so much that he had to drop the gun to pull her to her feet. She heard him mutter something she couldn't understand and she had a vivid moment's recognition of green eyes, no longer ice-cold but hard with a burning anger, as her head was pushed against his shoulder and her body, betrayingly, sank gratefully against solidly braced male muscles, taking the support they offered without paying the slightest heed to her brain's feverish command to resist and pull away.

Dimly she was aware of the doors opening, of hurried, staccato conversation; her eyes fluttered open, to discover that she was still holding the baby and that both of them were safe and unharmed.

The arms that had been holding her fell away and she told herself it was foolish to experience such an acute sense of loss. Dizzily she became aware of her surroundings; of the limp, lifeless dark-suited bodies lying on the floor; of the small, voluable middle-aged man who had erupted into the room, and whose features she vaguely recognised; but most of all of the man who had been holding her and who was now standing several feet away talking calmly to his plump, disturbed companion, both of them pausing to glance at Claire.

She only realised when the baby let out a protesting cry that she was holding him too tightly. Her head felt as though it was full of cotton wool. She seemed to have strayed into another world and she still couldn't take in what had happened. Now, only the overturned table and the smashed crockery remained to prove that it had been real, that she had actually taken shelter behind it while bullets flew about the room. Suddenly, desperately, she wanted to laugh—or to cry—and the only thought surfacing through the muddle of her brain was that if she had to pay for the broken china it would probably use all her godmother's parting cheque.

'Please . . . forgive me . . . I am so disturbed that I forget my manners.' Claire smiled vaguely at the plump bearded man. 'I am Sheikh Ahmed ibn Hassan,' he told her, introducing himself, 'and if you had not . . .' He tried to compose himself, shaking his head slowly. 'Allah must have been smiling upon us this morning, Miss . . .'

Dutifully Claire supplied her name. 'But, we cannot talk of this here. Will you come up to my suite so that I can thank you more properly . . .?' He saw her hesitation and smiled, warmth and charm lighting his rather heavy features, and in that instant Claire recognised him.

He was the head of a small Middle Eastern state and she had seen his photograph in the papers. He was in Britain on a state visit, although the Press had suggested there might be something more in it than that. His country would offer a strategic point for Europe and its allies in a military sense, and it was strongly hinted that this could be the purpose underlining his visit. Claire also remembered reading that his nephew and heir had recently been killed in an accident together with his wife, and there had been rumblings of a Soviet plot to instate a ruler of their choice with sympathies to them rather than to the West.

'I can ask the hotel management to vouch for me . . .' her companion was saying earnestly and Claire realised that he had misinterpreted her hesitation.

She shook her head and proffered a brief smile. 'No . . . no. I recognise you from your photograph in the papers, Sheikh.'

When they left the room they were followed by most of the other occupants, although Claire noticed that one man stayed behind and the mockery in his green eyes seemed to follow her as she walked out of the room, head held high, the baby still clutched in her arms, surrounded by what seemed like a phalanx of silent men.

The lavishness of the Sheikh's suite made her blink, and as she sat down Claire found herself wondering curiously about the child she was still cuddling. She couldn't blot out of her mind looking up and seeing that gun pointed lethally in the direction of the highchair.

'You must be wondering what is going on,' Sheikh Ahmed announced when she had refused a cup of coffee and his attendants had been dismissed. 'This child,' he looked at the baby on her knee, 'is the only son of my nephew, and will in time succeed me as ruler of our state. Today's events have proved beyond any shadow of a doubt that his life is at risk.' The baby started to cry and he frowned in concern. 'There is something wrong?'

Claire shook her head wryly. 'Not really. He is wet and hungry. His nursemaid . . . the girl who was with him in the dining-room . . .'

'I suspect she was a plant who had been paid to leave him unattended. He is normally guarded at all times, but Raoul tells me that the girl insisted that I had said he was to eat in the dining-room. This is not true, and if it had not been for your quick actions . . .'

'I thought we were both going to die,' Claire admitted, shuddering herself.

'And yet thinking that, you did not abandon Saud,' the Sheikh commented watching her. 'Raoul tells me that but for your quick thinking Saud would be dead.'

'Were you . . . were you expecting something to happen?' Claire asked, remembering the guns which had appeared as though by magic in the hands of the men in the dining-room.

The Sheikh shrugged fatalistically. 'Not so much expecting as suspecting. There is a faction in our country that does not approve of our ties with the West. It is not always easy to know friend from foe and one must always be on one's guard. Saud's nursemaid is an example of how easy it is to be deceived. I myself am widowed and have no female relatives close enough to trust with the child.' He suddenly looked tired and careworn. 'But I must not

burden you with our problems. I should like to reward
you for . . .'

'No . . .' Claire spoke quickly and automatically,
reiterating, 'no . . . please, I would rather you did not.
I simply acted instinctively.' She looked down at the
child now sleeping on her lap. 'Is there someone who
can change and feed him?' It seemed incredible to her
that this child, who was apparently so important,
should have no one to care properly for him.

'I had hoped to find a nanny for him while we are
here, but Raoul is opposed to it. He believes Saud
would be better looked after by one of our own race.'
He smiled. 'Perhaps because of his own dual blood,
Raoul is more opposed to Saud having a foreign nanny
than might otherwise be the case. He feels very deeply
the differences which set him aside from his peers.'

What relationship did Raoul have with the baby on
her lap, Claire wondered, but it was a question she
could not ask, she had no desire to pry into the
personal life of the man who had looked at her so
coldly with those too-seeing green eyes. Had they
registered her minute, betraying reaction to his
proximity? The momentary weakness which had had
nothing at all to do with her shock and had instead
sprung from an entirely voluntary response to him as
an intensely male man? It was humiliating to think
that they might, especially when she had on more than
one occasion seen the derisive dismissal of her as a
woman in his eyes.

'Er . . .' She paused, seeing hesitation and embarrassment on the Sheikh's face, intrigued because she
sensed it wasn't a habitual expression for him.

'Saud's room is through there.' He indicated a

communicating door. 'Would it be trespassing too much to ask you to . . .?'

'You want me to change and feed him?' Claire supplemented, hiding a small smile.

'We did not bring a large entourage; the boy's nursemaid was to have been sufficient. I feared to leave him behind unprotected, but now . . . I think what happened this morning will prove to Raoul that we cannot entrust his care to anyone lightly. The girl who had charge of him came extremely highly-recommended, and yet it is plain that she was part of the plot to kill him.'

Remembering how the girl had lost her temper with the child, and looked so pointedly at her watch before she left the dining-room, Claire suspected that he was right.

The Sheikh was charming and as she allowed herself to be manoeuvred into taking Saud into his own bedroom to attend to his needs, she repressed a small smile. This was most definitely not what her godmother had had in mind for her stay in London.

The baby was supplied with every luxury imaginable, from toys to silk and satin clothes, but there seemed to be scant love in his young life, Claire thought pityingly as she first fed and then bathed him. He was not a difficult baby really, responding affectionately to her when she cuddled and held him. She was just towelling him dry, laughing as he lay gurgling on her lap, when the door opened. She tensed automatically, unable to blot out the mental image of men carrying guns and the high-pitched whine of bullets.

Cool green eyes surveyed her speculatively. 'A very

domesticated picture. What a shame that it is me and not Ahmed who is witnessing it. What are you hoping for with this touching display of maternalism, Miss Miles? More than a diamond bracelet, obviously.'

Claire winced, recognising that he had overheard her conversation with her godmother the previous night, and then anger replaced embarrassment as she recognised the calculated insult behind his words. He was implying that she was motivated by materialism. Her full pink lips tightened ominously, and for a moment she considered thrusting the still damp baby into his arms and letting him finish the task for himself. That would soon destroy his sardonic dignity. A small giggle bubbled up inside her as she pictured his immaculately suited figure dealing with the squirming baby.

'Sheikh Ahmed asked if I would help, and I agreed,' she said calmly, 'but only because Saud was both wet and hungry, and too small yet to fend for himself. Sheikh Ahmed tells me that you are against his employing a European nanny for Saud.'

'You *have* been exchanging confidences, haven't you? What else did he tell you?'

'Nothing.'

'Liar. I'm sure knowing my uncle as I do that he also told you of my mixed blood, and now, no doubt, you are on fire with curiosity to know more.'

His arrogance provoked her into an instinctive anger. 'On the contrary,' she told him coldly, 'I have no desire to know the slightest thing about you. Why should I?' She finished buttoning Saud into clean rompers and got up, thrusting the baby towards him, a little surprised by how deftly he held the child, then swept out of the room before he could stop her, seething with fury, because he was right—she had been curious about him. Of course, he must be used to women finding him fascinating. That blend of East and West was a potent one, and he knew it, damn him!

She had always loathed arrogant, self-assured men, Claire reminded herself as she let the door slam behind her and hurried towards the lift, and if she had responded momentarily to the sheer male power of his body against her, it had been a reaction intensified by weakness and relief. After all, she would be a fool to think for one moment that those green eyes might burn with tenderness and passion for her, or that that hard, faintly cruel mouth might touch hers in need and hunger. A complete fool.

CHAPTER TWO

THERE was no reason for her to feel so dissatisfied. Her day had passed pleasantly enough, Claire told herself. She had visited the Tate to admire many old favourites, and then there had been a pleasant walk through the park. Now she was on her way back to the Dorchester to indulge herself with afternoon tea in the promenade room, so why should she feel this tiny feathering of restlessness that kept disturbing her? Perhaps it was because she was alone. She would write to Teddy, send him a postcard of the hotel. Thinking of Teddy reminded her of her ever-present worries about finding his school fees. Generous though her salary was, it couldn't cover them. She would have to find a part-time job. By her reckoning, she could just about manage two more terms with what savings they had left, and the present term's were paid.

'Afternoon tea, madam?' The waiter's voice broke into her reverie, and when she nodded he showed her to a comfortable padded chair, the small table in front of her set for two.

It was just gone five o'clock, obviously a popular time for tea, because most of the tables were taken, and Claire amused herself as she waited for hers to be brought by studying her surroundings. The room itself was long and rectangular with several sets of doors leading off it which she knew led to the restaurants. Decorated in soft buttercup-yellow with the frieze picked out in gold, the decor was an attractive one. Marble columns soared up to the ceiling, and underfoot was a soft patterned carpet rather like an Aubusson. Voices rose and fell mingling with the chink of china cups and the clatter of cutlery against plates.

Nibbling her dainty sandwiches, Claire continued her scrutiny. Expensively and elegantly dressed men and women sat at the small tables, couples in the main, although there were some family groups. All at once she felt very alone, the food she was eating turning to sawdust in her mouth. Pushing away her plate, Claire got up unsteadily, the events of the morning catching up with her. The Head Porter handed her her key when she asked for it, and also an envelope bearing her name. Unable to recognise the handwriting, Claire frowned as she headed for the lift, the small mystery solved when she opened the envelope and realised that the letter was from Sheikh Ahmed.

The lift came. She was the sole passenger and started to read her letter as she was borne upwards. Barely able to take in its contents before the lift stopped, she hurried to her room, unlocking the door with nervous fingers, sinking down into the comfortable chair by the window before unfolding the heavy, expensive paper and reading through the note again.

The Sheikh wanted to see her to discuss something with her. But what? The note was almost deliberately evasive, full of gratitude for what she had done and yet really telling her nothing of the Sheikh's purpose in writing to her. He would send someone to escort her to his suite, his note informed her. Obviously she wasn't going to be allowed to refuse.

Repressing a sigh, Claire found the card she had bought for Teddy and started to write to him. The summer holidays were coming up and she already knew that Teddy had been invited to join a schoolfriend on his father's yacht. She had been worrying about how she was going to pay for the clothes that he would need, but her godmother's generous cheque had solved that problem. It would also enable her to give Teddy some money of his own to spend while he was away and she was just writing to him to this effect when she heard the sharp rap on her door. Guessing in advance that it would be one of Sheikh Ahmed's armed men, she went to the door and opened it, suppressing a small stunned gasp of dismay when she realised he had sent Raoul.

'I'll just get my bag and my key,' she told him, surprised to find that he was following her into her room. Her key and bag were on the far bed and as she picked them up she was astounded to discover that Raoul was openly reading the card she had been writing to Teddy.

'Your lover?' he questioned, without a hint of embarrassment at being discovered.

'My relationship with Teddy is private,' Claire responded furiously. From the first moment she had set eyes on him something about this man had antagonised her, and it was plain that he shared her antipathy. He was looking at her with something that bordered on acute dislike.

'That will be something my uncle hasn't bargained for,' he murmured under his breath as he straightened up, but before Claire could question him further he was heading for the door, the small courtesy of opening it for her and then standing back so that she could precede him, drawing a thin, sardonic smile from his lips. 'My mother used to say that the thing that made her fall in love with my father was his good manners. My countrymen . . .'

'Believe in treating their women like possessions,' Claire said unwisely. 'No wonder your mother chose to marry a European.'

'You prefer European males to Eastern?' The dark eyebrows shot up. 'Why is that, I wonder? Because you know it is easier to dominate them? Are you then a modern, liberated woman, Miss Miles, who believes herself equal or indeed superior to my sex? A woman who chooses her lovers as her grandmother might have done a new gown and discards them just as easily . . .'

Trying to hold on to her temper, Claire responded briefly, 'And you? Am *I* to infer from what you have said that you prefer your women to be of a more biddable disposition; Muslim women, in fact, taught from the cradle to revere and worship the dominant male? How fortunate we both are that we can indulge our separate tastes without opposition.'

She had meant the words as a taunt, but had been totally unprepared for the look of dark, almost brooding anger that tightened every feature, his eyes almost black as they bored into puzzled grey ones.

'You might be able to indulge your preferences, Miss Miles,' he said at last, 'I am less fortunate. Muslim fathers are careful where they bestow their daughters, and like any child of a dual-race marriage, I am totally accepted by neither. Indeed, if it were not for the good offices of my uncle Sheikh Ahmed, I doubt I would even have a country to call my own.' He saw her expression and his face hardened further. 'You might find the thought of a marriage between East and West a romantic concept, Miss Miles,' he told her, correctly reading her thoughts, 'but my mother soon discovered to her cost that my father had no intention of keeping the promises he made when they became man and wife. In the East at least a woman has the comfort of her family if she should be deserted or ill-treated by her husband, in the West . . . My father married my mother purely for her wealth. Once they were married and I was conceived, he devoted all his spare time to other women and gambling. My mother died shortly after I was born. The shame of her husband's desertion was something she could no longer endure, and once my father discovered that he was not going to benefit from his marriage, he gave my uncle the option of either bringing me up himself or placing me in an orphanage.'

Why was he telling her this? Only this morning he had savaged her with the knife thrust of his contempt for merely betraying a brief curiosity, but now he was telling her the intimate details of his life, and in such a taut, bitter way that she guessed every word was a sharp thorn piercing an old wound. She couldn't understand it.

They were borne upwards in the lift towards the Sheikh's private suite. As before, the Sheikh was alone, his smile welcoming and she was sure sincere, as he waved her into a chair.

'Please, sit down, Miss Miles,' he glanced at his

nephew as Claire obediently sank into a plush chair. 'Has Raoul said anything to you of my purpose in asking you to join us?'

'I have told her nothing. You know my views.'

'But if she is agreeable you will . . .'

'I will do whatever is needed to protect the child, you know that.'

Alarmed by the harsh tone of his voice and the undercurrents she could sense seething between the two men, Claire glanced from Raoul's set, dark face to the Sheikh's kinder, but no less resolute one.

'You are alarming our guest, Raoul,' he berated mildly. 'My dear, there is no need to be afraid. Indeed we are the ones to suffer that emotion lest you should . . .' He broke off while Claire stared up at him in mystification. Neither of them struck her as men who would fear anything, especially Raoul. By his actions this morning he had proved that when it came to physical danger . . . She shuddered, suddenly overtaken by a vivid memory of the gunmen and the rapid sound of gunfire, the fear that had been pushed aside by the adrenalin-induced need to act now emerging to surge sickeningly through her veins. Only the knowledge that Raoul was watching her and would no doubt relish her weakness gave her the strength to suppress her feelings, her nerves as taut as fine wire as she waited for the Sheikh to continue.

'I have a proposition to put to you, Miss Miles,' he began quietly, and beneath the calm dignity of his manner Claire sensed a deep inner disquietude. 'Indeed, it is only because I sense within you a warm and sympathetic personality that I am able to speak of this matter to you at all.' He gave her a charming smile. 'You might say that I am taking an unfair advantage of your good nature, and I'm afraid that is true. This morning you risked your own life to save that of my nephew . . .'

'I acted entirely instinctively,' Claire told him, a faint warm colour staining her cheekbones. If the Sheikh had brought her here to offer her another reward, she was going to refuse it. But surely a reward would not necessitate Raoul's presence or be the cause of the uncertainty and agitation she sensed in the older man?

'Perhaps, but nevertheless, your first instinct was to protect Saud, and I myself have observed your care of the child. You like children, Miss Miles?'

'Yes, but . . .' Her voice trailed off as her muddled thoughts clarified. Could the Sheikh be going to ask her to act as Saud's nanny? 'I could not look after him full-time if that is what you are about to suggest. I have a job already, and then . . .' Then there was Teddy, but some inner caution made her say haltingly, 'I have certain commitments . . .'

'To your lover?' Raoul suggested sardonically. 'His should be the commitment to you, Miss Miles.'

'There is a man already in your life?' The Sheikh looked disturbed.

'Yes . . .'

'But you are not betrothed or married to him. There is no truly firm commitment?'

Her mouth had gone dry. Why hadn't she simply explained that Teddy was her brother right from the start? How on earth was she going to extricate herself from her own half-truths now? Anger came to her rescue. What business was it of either of these men what her relationship with Teddy was?

'Miss Miles and her lover are conducting a long-distance affair,' Raoul supplemented cynically. 'She was writing to him when I went to collect her.'

'So . . . Then it is possible that you would be free to return with us to Omarah?'

'As Saud's nanny? I cannot. I am not trained . . . I . . .'

'It is not as Saud's nanny that my uncle requires your services, Miss Miles,' Raoul cut in in a hatefully mocking voice, 'but as his mother.'

'His mother?' The room seemed to whirl dizzily in front of her eyes, 'but . . . but that is impossible.'

'Biologically yes, but . . .'

'What my nephew is trying to say, Miss Miles, is that in order to protect Saud it might be as well if we allowed those who instigated this morning's attack to believe it succeeded. No . . . please hear me out,' he begged when Claire would have interrupted. 'No one apart from ourselves and my guards, whose loyalty I know I can depend on, know the truth. Those sent to kill my nephew have themselves been killed, but if we return to Omarah with Saud there will be other attempts on his life, attempts which could easily prove to be successful, and then I fear my country will turn its eyes and heart to Russia. You know already of the divisions in my country.' He drew a sharp sigh. 'Had Raoul been the son of my brother rather than the son of my sister, I could have appointed him as my heir . . .'

'And that, I believe, is the only thing I can thank my father for,' Raoul interrupted grimly.

'I know you have no wish to step into my shoes, Raoul. Raoul is the head of our petrochemical industries,' the Sheikh told Claire, and something in the look on the former's face told her that this was no sinecure post, and that Raoul was completely genuine when he said that he had no wish to take his uncle's place.

'And thanks to the insistence of my father I am also a Christian,' Raoul added grittily. He saw Claire's look of surprise and said cuttingly, 'Does it surprise you to know that those of my uncle's faith are so tolerant towards others? The Prophet himself decreed that it must be so.'

Why, when he obviously felt so bitter about his father, and had chosen to ally himself to the Arab blood he carried, had he not changed his religion, Claire wondered, trying to shrug her curiosity aside as the Sheikh shook his head warningly.

'We digress Raoul. We have not appraised Miss Miles of our . . . plan. Obviously, if we do allow it to be known that Saud did not survive this morning's attack, it would be difficult for us to take the child back with us to Omarah. I did think at one time of leaving him in your country where he could be brought up in secret and, I hope, in safety, but . . .'

'But if you do that he will grow up a stranger to his own country and its customs. The people would never accept him in your place. He would be more European than Arab.'

'This is true,' the Sheikh agreed gravely, 'which is why, my dear, we are seeking your help. You see, the only way we can take Saud back with us in safety is if we take him as someone else's child. You can see, I am sure, the dangers attendant on such a course. How could we be sure that the couple we might choose would be trustworthy? And Saud must be brought up as befits his station.'

'I am honoured that you should have thought of me as a candidate,' Claire responded truthfully, 'but surely, even if I agreed, people would think it strange that you should take into your family an unmarried European girl with a child. Surely they would suspect . . .'

The two men exchanged a look that made her blood turn to ice in her veins, a feeling that she had suddenly strayed on to very unsteady ground sending alarm signals rushing to her brain.

'I have not entirely explained, Saud would not just be your child, but . . . but Raoul's as well. It would be announced that you were married during our visit to your country, and . . .'

'Oh, but that couldn't possibly work,' Claire expostulated, refusing to dwell for the moment on the multitude of sensations assailing her and clinging only to the bare facts. Later, when she was alone, she would allow herself to think more deeply on the strange sensation stirring in the pit of her stomach at the thought of Raoul as her husband . . . her lover.

The look he gave her was bitterly sardonic. 'Well, it won't,' she said sharply. 'Everyone will know that we haven't been married long enough to have a child, and . . . and with a European woman . . . Surely . . .'

Finding no reassurance in Raoul's hard, cynical features, she looked wildly at the Sheikh, her heart sinking at what she saw in his calm, dark eyes.

'We have been into this, and if you are in agreement, our story will be that Saud was the result of an affair between you and Raoul. He spends a considerable amount of time abroad, so that aspect need not cause us any concern. Your child will have been born illegitimately, and I will have coerced Raoul into marriage with you, for the child's sake.'

The picture he was painting wasn't a very attractive one and Claire found herself grimacing in distaste. 'I suspect Miss Miles is thinking the proposition would sound more attractive had I been the one to do the coercing, Uncle,' Raoul interceded mockingly, 'but you are not thinking clearly, Miss Miles. No one knowing me would believe that I had willingly married a European woman . . .'

'But they will believe that one bore your child?' Their argument had personal undertones that bewildered Claire. Calm and even-tempered, she had never allowed herself to be so provoked and disturbed by any man. In fact, she had come to think of herself as someone who could not be affected physically by men, and yet this man with merely a look—a word— had inflamed her temper to the point where she could feel her self-control slipping dangerously away.

'I am a man who spends a considerable amount of time away from my own people,' Raoul acknowledged, shrugging as though dismissing her accusation as juvenile gaucheness. 'Naturally, it would not be expected that I should live as a monk. It is also well-known in our country that European women take lovers.'

'I cannot do it,' she said positively. 'I'm sorry, but I . . .' She broke off as the door opened and a young girl walked in carrying Saud. She was dressed in the uniform of the hotel staff, the little boy was still flushed and fretful. But he seemed to recognise Claire, perhaps because of her fair hair, which was probably unusual to him, Claire thought, unable to check her own response and he wriggled impatiently in the girl's hold, stretching out his arms to her.

The girl came over and handed Saud to her, saying something in Arabic that Claire couldn't understand, before leaving the room.

'She thinks you are Saud's mother,' the Sheikh pointed out quietly. 'I know it is a great deal to ask of you, but I beg you to reconsider. Saud's life is at stake ... We cannot protect him for every second of it. Another year and we shall have overcome our problems. Then you will be free to go. A year, that is all we ask.'

'And, of course, you will be well paid,' Raoul interjected swiftly, mentioning a sum of money that made Claire gasp. It was a fortune, more than enough to put Teddy through school and university and still leave enough for her to buy herself a small house instead of the poky flat she presently rented.

'But ... marriage ...'

'Our marriage will be a mere fiction,' Raoul assured her contemptuously. 'Why else do you think my uncle is at such pains to state that it will have been forced upon me? That way neither of us will be expected to play too false a part. We can live our separate lives ... I told you you should have offered the money first,' he said over her head to his uncle.

The contempt and ugly suggestiveness of his tone took Claire's breath away. She dearly longed to throw his words back in his face, and his money, but at that moment Saud started to cry, and by the time she had soothed him, rocking the small round body against her shoulder, enjoying the warm baby smell of him, she had

had time to think. Time to consider all that such a large sum of money could mean for Teddy. No more scrimping and scraping; no more having to do without the treats enjoyed by most of his fellow boarders. She suppressed a small sigh, knowing that she really had no choice. And then there was Saud. Already she was fond of the small child. There had been one attempt on his life, and she had to admit that the Sheikh's plan was an excellent one.

'I ... I agree.' The words almost choked in her throat as she saw Raoul's cynically knowing eyes rest on her flushed cheeks. The Sheikh was thanking her profusely, but Claire barely heard him, she was still too shaken by the look of acute dislike she could see in Raoul's eyes. And this was the man she would have to live with as his wife for twelve months! It was on the tip of her tongue to take back her words, but before she could speak he forestalled her.

'I will have the arrangements put in hand. First we will fly to Paris. At the end of the week . . .'

'Paris?'

He saw her stunned expression and laughed sarcastically. 'Oh, don't worry, I have no intention of extending the farce of our "marriage" to include my French relatives, it is just that as my wife you will be expected to maintain a certain standard of dress and appearance.' His lips twisted bitterly as they surveyed her slender frame in the tailored tweed suit. 'While your clothes might be perfectly suitable for your present life-style . . .'

'My nephew is quite right,' the Sheikh interposed sympathetically when he saw her face. 'He is a very wealthy man, and it would not be fitting . . .'

'But surely, if everyone knows you have forced him to marry me, they will not expect . . .'

'What they will expect is for you to be dressed as befits my wife, even if I don't treat you as such.' He grimaced as he caught her brief flush, and added with infuriating accuracy, 'Oh come, surely you don't really suppose that I can't see what is running through your foolish head now? I will say this once and once only, Miss Miles. Even if you were the type of woman I find physically attractive, which you are not, the fact that you have another lover, and your very evident avarice, would undoubtedly be sufficient to kill any desire I might have for you.'

Claire went red and then white as he turned on his heel and stormed out of the room, leaving her alone with the Sheikh and Saud in a silence that seemed to thicken with every passing second.

'Try to forgive him,' the Sheikh said softly at last. 'His has not been an easy life. His mother, my sister, was forced to live almost as a servant in her own home when she returned from France. She had married Lucien D'Albro against my father's wishes, and when they parted . . .' He drew a faint sigh. 'You must understand that it is a matter of family honour when a woman parts from her husband, and my father was of the old school. To make matters worse, a marriage had been arranged for Zenobe. She died when Raoul was very young, but my father remained bitter about his birth to the end. As a child I remember Raoul desperately wanted to be accepted by my father, but he was a man of cruel pride. Raoul of all the family is most like him, and I think my father sensed this. Against his will he loved Raoul best of all his grandchildren. When he died he left him a considerable fortune, but nothing could wipe away the bitter loneliness of those early years. As a child, Raoul was taught to hate and deride his European inheritance. As an adult, he knows that this teaching sprang from my father's anger against Zenobe and against her husband, but Raoul is a complex character; a man who has suffered and still suffers great pain.'

He saw Claire's expression and assured her softly, 'You do not believe me, but I assure you this is so. Why else, now that he is an adult and free to adopt the Muslim religion if he so chooses, does he deny himself this thing that he wanted so desperately as a child? He is a man deeply conscious of the schisms within himself.'

Rather than reassuring her, the Sheikh's words only made her regret more than ever her folly in agreeing to accept the role of Raoul's wife. It might only be make-believe, but some deep inner instinct warned her against any sort of intimacy with Raoul, no matter how tenuous. He would hurt her if he could, she could sense it inside him. Saud stirred in her arms, and she glanced down at the olive face.

'Already he is attached to you,' the Sheikh said quietly. 'I should like you to remain here with us until it is time for you to leave for Paris.'

'I . . . I shall have to tell my employers.' And Teddy, she added mentally. She would drive down to his school to tell him—but tell him what? She nibbled her lip, worrying at its soft fullness, as she took Saud through to his own room and set about preparing his food. She knew that there were several Arab children at Teddy's school. If she told Teddy the truth, he might innocently mention it, and she felt it would be unfair to put the Sheikh's plans at risk. But what other alternatives did she have? She could hardly not tell her brother anything.

The problem worried at her mind as she prepared Saud for bed. Perhaps she ought to allow Teddy the fiction that she was marrying Raoul. She would say nothing of Saud, of course ... And then in twelve months' time? Marriages broke up all the time ... Dear God, what was she doing?

Panic swept over her, pushing aside all her sensible thoughts and decisions. She couldn't go through with it. She couldn't! She couldn't put herself in the power—no matter how briefly—of Raoul D'Albro. He would taunt and torment her continually. She had seen it in his eyes when they studied her with contempt and bitterness. But she had to go through with it. She had said she would—and then there was the money.

Her mouth twisted wryly. Oh, she had seen the look in Raoul's eyes when he mentioned it. He thought she had accepted through greed, but he was wrong—quite wrong. It was for Teddy's sake, not for her own personal gain. But he thought Teddy was her lover. As her feelings of panic subsided, Claire acknowledged that she was the one responsible for that error. But even if she could correct it, would she? Wasn't she safer while Raoul thought she was a greedy, avaricious female with at least one established lover?

But safe from what? Even if he knew the truth Raoul would not be interested in her. She wasn't his type. He had told her that. But the danger didn't come from him, it came from within herself, Claire acknowledged tiredly. Right from the very first time she had seen him it had been there, although she had fought against admitting it; she had told herself that he was everything she disliked and resented in a man.

And he was, but there was more to it than that; more to her feelings than mere dislike. And yes, if she were honest, she would have to admit to the faint, but unmistakable feelings of nervy excitement that his presence aroused. An excitement which she knew instinctively possessed the seeds of very great danger.

CHAPTER THREE

THE week seemed to fly past. Claire spent most of it with Saud, and found herself getting fonder and fonder of the little boy with every hour that passed. Fifty thousand pounds had been deposited in her bank account, and she had written to her employers, telling them that she was getting married, deeming this the wisest course in view of what she intended to tell Teddy.

Teddy. She gnawed anxiously on her lower lip. Yesterday she had told Raoul that she had someone she had to see before they left for Paris. From his cynical, taunting smile she knew he thought she referred to her lover, and she hadn't tried to correct him, but now, this morning, he had told her that a car and driver would be put at her disposal—in case she tried to run out on her agreement, she thought cynically. After all, with the money in her bank account . . . But no, she would never do that. She would keep her side of the bargain, for little Saud's sake if nothing else.

It would take about three hours to drive to Teddy's school, and somehow she would have to find a way of eluding her driver, just in case he discovered it wasn't a man she was seeing but a little boy! Perhaps she could persuade him to wait for her in the village. It was only a mile from the school. She could easily walk. Thank goodness she had had the foresight to telephone the school and speak to Teddy's headmaster. He had readily agreed to allow her to speak to Teddy, promising that he would warn her brother to expect her visit.

She had bought him a new watch, remembering that he needed one badly, and hoping that she had made the right choice. She was just studying it when her door opened and Raoul walked in. As always, she felt acutely ill at ease in his presence, her sense of anxiety increasing as his cool gaze slid over her slender body in its pale lemon linen suit. The suit was relatively new and fitted her body snugly, drawing attention to the slender curves of her hips and her slim length of thigh.

His mouth curled when he had finished his inspection. 'Very cool and correct. What are you hoping to do? Drive him into wanting the woman you have hidden behind the barrier of your oh so correct clothes?' His eyes sharpened as he saw the watch she was holding in her hand. 'What's this?'

'A farewell present,' Claire told him tautly, shivering beneath the icy glare of fury he directed towards her.

'You are giving him presents?' His mouth tightened ominously. 'Is the gift of your body not enough?' Anger gave way to contempt. 'Abase yourself as you wish, Claire Miles, while you bear your own name, but once you carry mine . . .' He broke off to study her contemptuously. 'Have you no pride that you must needs buy a man's affection with gifts? What does he give you, Claire, apart from satisfying you with his body? What manner of man is he?'

His mouth twisted with contempt, impelling Claire to retaliate, to wound his pride as he had tried to wound hers. 'What's the matter, Raoul?' she demanded, her voice husky with anger. 'Has no woman ever loved you enough to buy you gifts; to sacrifice her pride? Are you always the one who has to do the buying? Is that . . .'

'You will not speak to me like that.' He had closed the gap between them before she could move, his fingers biting painfully into the soft flesh of her upper arm, his eyes so dark that they seemed almost black, forcing her to stare helplessly into their mesmerising gaze as he dragged her against his body. She could feel the anger emanating from him, the taut control of his body bending hers like a bow.

She had pushed him too far. She could see it in the controlled fury of his face. In the tight muscles of his body as her own jarred against the hard impact; and now the cruel line of his mouth was approaching hers, hovering, waiting to punish. Something quivered through her, burning her skin, and her lips parted invitingly, her eyes soft and luminous. She caught Raoul's muttered imprecation and then suddenly she was free, dazed and bewildered to the point of shock.

'Oh no,' he was saying tightly. 'Oh no,' he reiterated with cruel softness. 'I'm not falling for that. What did you expect,' he added tauntingly watching her white face, 'that I would be deceived by your clumsy ploy? Enough to take you into my arms perhaps and from there into my bed? How much would I have had to pay for that dubious pleasure, I wonder? However cheap the price, it would be too much. You overrate your appeal and my need. Both would have to increase considerably before I would even contemplate such a course.'

'I . . .' Fury tied Claire's tongue in knots. And besides, how could she explain logically that moment-ary and totally bewildering impulse which had had her lifting her face to his, ignoring all the warning commands of her brain?

Humiliation scorched through her. Somehow she managed to stagger out of her room and into Saud's, picking up the little boy with arms that still trembled, hugging him as though somehow the warmth of his body would dispel the frozen bitterness that seemed to have invaded her every bone and muscle.

How could she go on with this charade, knowing how deeply and intensely Raoul despised her? But how could she not do it when she thought of what was at stake? And she wasn't thinking just of the money which she needed so badly. There was also Saud, of whom she had become very fond, and who she knew was daily becoming more attached to her. If Raoul's dislike and contempt was the only price she was asked to pay for Saud's safety and Teddy's future financial security, surely it was not too great a burden to bear?

It was just after eleven when she went downstairs to the foyer to find that her car and driver were waiting for her. The fact that the car was an elegant and brand-new Rolls caught her off guard and she stared uncertainly at it for a moment before approaching it cautiously. When the front passenger door was thrust open unceremoniously she eyed it uncertainly, gasping with shock and disbelief when Raoul's voice com-manded her curtly to 'Get in.'

'You!' Sheer disbelief prompted the shocked protest, but to judge from the tightening of his skin over the bones of his face, Raoul had read more than disbelief into her brief exclamation.

'Did you honestly expect I would allow you to see this man un . . .'

'Unguarded?' Claire supplied bitterly for him as she slid into the plush leather seat and closed the door after her. 'What's the matter? Are you afraid he might persuade me to change my mind?'

The look on Raoul's face as he turned towards her shocked her with its biting contempt. 'Hardly,' he drawled, his eyes pitiless as they raked over her pale face and slender body. 'A man who accepts expensive gifts from a woman, who allows her to do all the running and chasing, isn't going to be fool enough to place her virtue and his honour above money.'

'Meaning, of course, that you would never stoop to allow your women to do so,' Claire threw at him angrily, torn between humiliation and searing fury. How dare he judge her so contemptuously and on so little evidence! A man who could do that must surely hold the whole female sex in contempt.

Her mouth tightened. It was just as well she had discovered this side of him from the start. That way she was hardly likely to be dazzled by his handsome face and masculine body. She checked, tensing, her fingers on her seat-belt as the full import of her train of thought sank home. Of course she hadn't been in danger of falling for Raoul; he might be the epitome of every girl's idyllic romantic daydreams, but she wasn't stupid enough to believe those daydreams could be translated into real life.

'My "women" as you term them, are content to be what Allah ordained them to be.' Raoul's cold, soft voice broke into her thoughts, sending icy shivers rippling over her skin.

'Meaning that they know their place and are kept in it,' she taunted back. 'Bought and paid for, so that they are easy to discard when you are bored with them, is that it? Or is it they who grow tired of pandering to your vulnerable ego, Raoul? It takes a very special sort of man to accept a woman as his equal in life, capable of thinking and functioning for herself; a man who can appreciate what a woman must give up when she . . .'

'Gives herself to her lover? In the East we have a saying that man and woman are food and drink, each enhancing the other. In my country a woman is not ashamed to be a woman. She is content in her own role and does not seek to usurp that of the male.'

They had joined the main stream of traffic and Raoul broke off to ask Claire for directions. She told him where they were heading and kept silent as he manoeuvred the large car through the ceaseless flow of traffic. He drove well, neither uncertainly nor aggressively, and his consideration for other drivers and pedestrians was something that surprised her. He had been so arrogant and contemptuous where she was concerned that she had expected him to betray the same traits towards others.

It wasn't until they had left the London traffic behind them and were heading out in the direction of Teddy's school that Raoul picked up the threads of their earlier conversation. 'As my supposed "wife" a certain standard of behaviour will be expected of you,' he began without preamble, and without taking his eyes off the road, 'and now is as good a time as any to speak of this. In the East . . .'

'A woman is a man's possession?' Claire interrupted furiously. 'But you are forgetting that you have been forced to "marry" me by your uncle. We will lead completely separate lives, or so you told me. Feeling the way you do, I'm surprised you aren't already married. To some dutiful, biddable Muslim girl brought up to think of her father and then her husband as her master.'

Dead silence filled the car, and a quick glance into Raoul's face showed Claire a look of such brooding bitterness that her heart quailed a little. It was too late now to regret her lack of tact, and she was surprised when, instead of changing the subject, Raoul said curtly, 'There was to have been such a marriage, but it required that I should change my religion.'

'And you would not? But why? You obviously consider yourself more Eastern than Western. You were brought up there.'

'Sometimes a man needs to be accepted for himself alone,' was all Raoul would say, but it gave Claire something to think about as the powerful Rolls gobbled up the miles.

His comment pointed to a far greater sensitivity than she could ever have imagined he would possess, a need to be accepted that gnawed at her thoughts as she tried to fit together the complicated pieces of the puzzle that went to make up the man seated at her side. The Sheikh had warned her that Raoul found his dual inheritance a difficult one and for the first time she began to appreciate what the older man had meant. To the casual onlooker, Raoul was completely of the East, but that was merely the outward covering; what about the man inside the tawny skin, the man whose father had so contemptuously rejected his mother—so much so that she had returned to her own people, taking her child with her?

It was only as they neared Teddy's school that Claire ceased tussling with the problem, turning her thoughts instead to Teddy and how she was going to stop Raoul and her brother from meeting.

She and Teddy were very close, a result of their parents' death, and Teddy was intelligent enough to suspect the truth if she did not take great care to hide it from him. She had no wish for her brother to grow up under the burden of knowing she had sacrificed her pride and self-respect so that she could pay his school fees, and so she had already decided to tell Teddy that she loved Raoul. There would be time enough later to worry about explaining to him why she had returned to England, her supposed marriage over, but that was something she wasn't going to think about right now. Her first problem was to get rid of Raoul.

In the end it was surprisingly easy to arrange her 'escape'. Raoul insisted that they stop for lunch five miles outside the village, at a hotel Claire remembered being taken to with her parents. It was a large country house set in its own grounds, and ordinarily she would thoroughly have enjoyed the treat of eating there, but on the pretext of wanting to tidy herself up she slipped away to telephone for a taxi, nervously dreading Raoul's appearance with every second that passed as she waited for it to arrive.

Only when she was finally inside it and speeding away from the hotel, did she expel a sigh of relief, hoping that the note she had handed in to reception would find its way safely to Raoul. In it she had told him briefly that she would be gone for a couple of hours. If he did not choose to wait for her she had sufficient money to get herself back to London and, feeing more confident than she had done since leaving London that morning, Claire settled back in her seat, watching the familiar countryside flash past.

Teddy's school had once been the country seat of a wealthy Victorian landowner, and Claire was warmly welcomed into the Headmaster's panelled study by that august gentleman. She had told him briefly on the telephone of the reason for her visit, and after exchanging pleasantries with her, he suggested that she might like to join Teddy in the small sitting-room off his study where they could have some degree of privacy.

Although it had only been Christmas when she last saw her brother, Claire was amazed at the way he had shot up. He badly needed new trousers, and it took her several seconds to get used to the unusual sensation of noting this without the sinking feeling of despair which normally followed such an occurrence. Teddy greeted her warmly, but with a boyish insouciance which brought home to her how quickly he was growing up.

'The Head told me you were coming. Said you'd got something to tell me . . .'

Both of them were remembering how she had been the one to break the news to him of their parents' death and Claire smiled reassuringly. 'Nothing to worry about. I just wanted you to know that I'm getting married.'

In order to avoid confusion, she had made up her mind that she would stick as closely to the Sheikh's story as possible, and so she explained to Teddy that she had recently met Raoul and that they were to be married abroad, all of which he accepted without too many questions, his main concern being whether he could come out to Omarah to spend some of his summer holidays with her.

'We'll have to see,' Claire hedged, deftly turning the conversation to other channels, asking him about his proposed trip with his schoolfriend, and handing over to him the money she had brought with her. 'You'll need some new clothes,' she added practically. 'I'll have a word with Matron before I leave.'

Because they had so many overseas boarders the school was perfectly accustomed to replenishing its boarders' wardrobes and Claire envisaged no problems in this respect. Before she left, two hours later, she had managed to fit in a brief discussion with Matron who had assured her that she could safely leave everything in her capable hands. A final goodbye and thank you to the Headmaster completed her afternoon's work, and Claire would have been surprised had she known his thoughts as he watched her walk down the drive.

A brave girl, and a selfless one who had shouldered the responsibility of her younger brother with a courage he wished more of his pupils could imitate. Dr Harwarden was a wise and knowledgeable man and he only hoped he was mistaken in his fears that this marriage, arranged so suddenly, was being entered into for the right reasons. Not that he doubted Claire's motives, but he was concerned that she might sacrifice herself for others. He knew there had been financial problems following her parents' death, and of the close relationship between brother and sister. Sighing a little, he turned his attention back to the mound of papers on his desk, telling himself that Claire was old enough to make her own decisions.

Wrapped up in her own thoughts, it wasn't until she drew level with the school gates that Claire saw the Rolls parked on the other side of them, Raoul lounging back in the driver's seat. Her footsteps slowed instinctively, apprehension feathering along her spine. How had he known where to find her? Did he know about Teddy? It was only stubborn pride that had kept her from telling him the truth herself. Let him think the very worst of her if he wished, she wasn't going to be the one to show him the error of his ways.

Instinctively, she knew if she told him the truth, his condemnation of her would be much less harsh, but the way in which he had immediately leapt to the wrong conclusion had stung her pride. Was that honestly how he saw her? If so, then let him, and as she approached the gates Claire knew that she did not want him to know the truth. She would rather he thought the worst he possibly could of her. It was as though his contempt of her was a protective barrier between them, although why she should need its protection she wasn't quite sure.

As he saw her approach, Raoul opened the car door and came towards her to unfasten the gate. His unfailing politeness set her teeth on edge, as though his actions were designed somehow to underline his contempt for her.

'How did you know where to find me?'

His eyebrows rose fractionally as she spoke. 'It

wasn't very difficult. I simply checked with the taxi firm. So your lover is a teacher. Is that why he doesn't mind you leaving him for a year, because it is difficult for the two of you to meet? What will you do with the money my uncle is paying you for acting the part of my wife? Help him to find more congenial employment?'

Expelling her breath on a faint sigh of relief, Claire refused to rise to his taunts. At least he didn't know the truth. 'I think that's my business, don't you?' she said loftily as she followed him back to the car, stopping in her tracks as Raoul suddenly came to a halt in front of her, grasping her chin with his fingers and tilting it upwards so that he could study her face.

'It must have been a very cool leave-taking,' he said slowly at last. His thumb brushed slowly against the fullness of her lower lip. 'Your mouth doesn't even look as though it has been kissed.'

Shock widened her eyes, her cheeks flushed as she wrenched herself free of his grasp. 'I don't think that's any of your business either, do you?' she asked icily, reaching for the door handle. 'Or is that the sort of thing that turns you on? Hearing about other people's . . .'

The ferocity of the expletive that left Raoul's lips cut across her words, and her body tensed automatically as she shrank away from him. 'Your innuendos are an insult,' he told her harshly, 'and no doubt the product of a silly, immature mind. Remember that from now on to all intents and purposes you are my wife, and you will be expected to behave accordingly.'

'By obeying your every word and abasing myself before you like . . . like a slave?'

The icy contempt in his eyes made her tremble at her folly in goading him. 'By remembering that I value my self-respect, even if you don't value yours, and that as my wife, my honour and good name *are* yours, and that any attempt to sully either will be swiftly punished.'

It was enough to keep her silent until they were well on the way back to London. Once or twice she stole a quick peep at his arrogant profile, each time reading a rejection and contempt there that reinforced her silence. If he didn't want to talk to her then he needn't. There was still much she would need to know about their life together; about his family, and how she would be expected to behave, but she wasn't going to beg to be told.

It was a relief to get back to the Dorchester, and the now familiar routine of caring for Saud. The little boy was openly pleased to see her, but Claire was conscious of Raoul's eyes boring into her back as she picked Saud up and cuddled him.

'Someone should tell your lover how good you are with children,' he murmured against her ear as she straightened up. She hadn't realised he was so close to her and Claire felt almost suffocated by the warmth of him against her back, a primitive flood of awareness burning through her body as it responded to the proximity of his. 'Or doesn't he care enough for you to give you the gift of his child?'

Only by pretending she hadn't heard him and keeping her back to him was Claire able to cope with the heat she could feel burning against her skin, unaware that she was still holding her breath in apprehension until the door closed behind him and she was safe to breathe out and relax.

'Would you care for a drink?' Claire couldn't help noticing that the air stewardess's smile for her was nowhere near as warm as it had been for Raoul. They were flying over the English Channel en route for Paris, Saud in between them, fast asleep. She had fought against this visit to Paris, but the Sheikh had gently pointed out the necessity of it to her. In their absence, the news of their marriage could be broken and would doubtless be picked up by the Press. Their trip to Paris would give Claire an opportunity to get used to her new role, and although she had protested that no man being forced into a marriage he did not want would take his new bride on a shopping spree in Paris, both Raoul and the Sheikh had overruled her.

'As my wife you will be expected to maintain a certain standard,' Raoul had repeatedly told her, adding sardonically, 'besides, you cannot really expect me to believe that any woman would turn down an opportunity to refurbish her entire wardrobe at a man's expense.'

'That depends on how she has to repay him,' Claire had retorted tartly, and as she relived the scene, she remembered how the Sheikh had smiled, half-secretly to himself as he listened to their quarrel. It was just as well that his plan did not call for her to play the adoring new bride, because that was something she was sure she would not be able to do.

Two hours later, installed in a luxurious suite at the George V, Claire was still trying to come to terms with the luxury of her surroundings. Unashamedly lavish, decorated with Flemish tapestries, sculptures, paintings and ormolu clocks, its magnificence took Claire's breath away. Delicate eighteenth-century French furniture, almost too dainty to use, furnished their suite. Her own bedroom could easily have housed a small apartment and the bathroom off it was a sybarite's dream. A cot had been provided for Saud and Claire's first duty was to feed and change the small boy. She was glad of the activity to take her mind off the fact that she and Raoul were now practically alone, Raoul having told his uncle that he thought it best that they dispensed with any retainers or guards for their trip to Paris.

'If we are to be accepted as a married couple it is necessary that we have a little time to ourselves to get used to the new role,' he had told the Sheikh, and trying to come to terms with her sudden elevation to the world of the unbelievably rich, Claire was glad that the Sheikh had allowed him to have his way. It was bad enough trying to behave as though such luxury was an everyday habit, without trying to cope with the curiosity of Raoul's retainers. Only a very few of the Sheikh's private staff were aware of the deception, mainly those men who had been in the dining-room when the murder attempt took place. It was fortunate that Saud was too young to talk yet, Claire ruminated as she changed him and placed him in the cot, otherwise the small boy might easily have betrayed them.

A member of the hotel staff was summoned to keep watch over the cot; as their child, Saud was in no danger, Raoul had told her, but even so, Claire knew a certain sense of misgiving when she joined Raoul in their sitting-room. For the flight he had worn a dark, formal suit, easily at home in European clothing, the white silk shirt drawing attention to the smooth dark texture of his skin. In the melding of East and West, he seemed to have inherited the best physical characteristics of both races, his features reminding Claire sharply of a Leonardo drawing or the purity of a Greek statue. He was almost too physically perfect, and in some ways it was no wonder he held her sex in contempt. He would have been hopelessly spoiled by it from the hour of his birth, even had fortune not favoured him with position and wealth in addition to good looks.

In silence she accompanied him to the lift and down into the foyer. In the taxi, Raoul spoke in fluid French, a sharp reminder of his parentage.

The rest of the day passed in a whirl of activity. If she had ever doubted the power of money, she did so no longer, Claire thought cynically as the staff of exclusive fashion houses fluttered round her like bees to honey, praising her slender figure, and the silver blondeness of her hair as they vied with one another to provide the sort of trousseau her new husband's wealth demanded.

Claire wasn't entirely surprised to learn that wealthy Arab women made up a large proportion of their clientele, but she firmly refused the ornate and lavish gowns that several of the couturiers told her were favourites with Middle Eastern women. Her own choice was for simple, well-cut clothes, and she was surprised to discover that Raoul seemed to share her taste. When she protested that she was hardly likely to wear half of the clothes he had selected, he cut her short, telling her curtly that contrary to her apparent belief they would be invited to many social events and that she would be expected to be dressed accordingly.

'As Finance Minister for our country I often have to entertain foreign dignitaries. As my wife, you will be representing our country on those occasions.' But that did not entirely soothe her conscience, especially when Raoul presented her with jewellery which must have cost a minor fortune. Emeralds and diamonds comprised a suite which would cover every occasion, the deep glow of the gems enhancing the colour of her eyes as they widened in awed disbelief over the glittering stones.

Exhausted long before the afternoon was over, it was only pride that kept Claire from pleading that they finished their shopping another day. Her feet ached and her head buzzed as she tried to assimilate all the differing experiences. It was like trying to digest too much rich food all in one go, and when Raoul took her elbow and escorted her into yet another discreetly expensive boutique, Claire was almost too numb to glance at her surroundings. It was only the sudden realisation that it was underwear that was being displayed for her consideration this time that jolted her out of her exhausted lethargy.

Delicate bras and briefs in finest silk and lace were displayed for his inspection, cool pretty cottons and openly seductive silk-satins in soft misty pastels and rich darker fabrics. The *vendeuse* barely concerned herself with Claire's opinion. A tall, elegant Frenchwoman in her thirties, all her concentration was centred on Raoul. And why not? Claire thought bitterly, he was the one paying the bills, buying for her the most intimate of clothes with a casual experience that spoke volumes on his knowledge of her sex.

'These, I think,' he ordered, indicating a camisole and matching french knickers in pale aqua silk-satin, lavishly trimmed with blonde lace. 'The colour will suit my wife's pale skin . . .'

'The fabric may not be suitable for a hot climate,' the vendeuse pointed out, glancing briefly at Claire. 'Cotton . . .'

In response Raoul picked up the silk-satin he had pointed out, letting the material slide smoothly from his fingers. 'Cotton does not feel like this,' he said coolly, his eyes registering the hot colour stealing over Claire's skin. An inner voice reminded her that for all his Eastern outlook he was a man who was part French; a sensualist, she guessed, no matter how much he might keep that side of his nature sternly controlled. Just for a moment she was tormented by an image of those lean, dark fingers against her skin, stroking it with the same appreciation with which he touched the silk, and then the vision was banished, her body trembling in acute reaction. How would she feel right now if Raoul was in fact her lover, was in fact buying her these clothes because he wanted to enjoy the warmth of her skin beneath its satin covering?

'Raoul, I don't need those . . .' she began jerkily, trying to dismiss her unruly thoughts, but her protest was ignored, and by the time they left the shop she felt she had enough new clothes to last her the rest of her life. She ought to have hated Raoul buying her such intimate items of clothing, but instead she felt almost excited, a strange, tense sensation invading the pit of her stomach.

What on earth was the matter with her? Raoul despised her. She must never allow herself to forget that fact. Raoul despised her and was simply playing a part.

By the time they returned to their hotel, Claire was so tired that she could only nod her head when Raoul suggested that they dine in their suite. Her meal tasted like sawdust as she envisioned all the lonely months ahead when the silence between them would stretch into what was becoming a familiar tension, or when she would be left completely alone while Raoul pursued his business interests. But what else did she expect? She was doing a job for which she was being paid extremely well and that was all there was to it. It was foolish to feel regret because Raoul evinced no desire for her company, or chagrin because he excused himself as soon as he had finished eating, retiring to his own room where she heard him lift the telephone and then talk into it in harsh Arabic.

Tired though she was, it seemed hours before sleep finally claimed her, her dreams a jumbled mixture of events from which she was glad to wake when the maid brought her a tray of tea and some small, plain biscuits, English and French newspapers on her tray.

Their marriage was mentioned in both; a discreet paragraph in *The Times* and something similar in its French equivalent. The gossip columns of the English tabloids gave a little more detail, including a mention of Saud. Unwittingly, Claire sighed. It was too late to back out now. For the next months at least she was, to all intents and purposes, Raoul's wife and Saud's mother.

Movements from the cot at her bedside reminded her of Saud's presence and she reached him just as he started to make his protest. His face was faintly

flushed, the gums he exposed to Claire in a wide grin
betraying the fact that another tooth was on the way.
Sitting on the side of her bed with him, Claire rubbed
his swollen gum consolingly. She would have to try
and buy him a teething ring. It constantly amazed her
that such a wealthy and important child should be so
lacking in the most basic comforts. If his mother had
lived things would have been different, and she told
herself that if nothing else, at least her presence would
benefit Saud.

She was so engrossed in watching him that she
didn't hear her bedroom door open, only becoming
aware of Raoul's presence when he was halfway across
the floor. Already up and dressed, he made her feel
acutely vulnerable in her thin cotton nightdress, her
hair still tousled and her face completely free of make-
up.

'You've seen the papers?' Claire nodded, still trying
to comfort Saud. 'What's the matter? Is something
wrong with him?' Raoul asked her, glancing down at
the child in her arms. Saud wriggled on her lap, his
movements tightening her nightdress until the soft
swell of her breasts was clearly visible beneath it.
Raoul's glance lingered only briefly on her body, but it
left Claire's acutely aware of her near-nudity.

'He's teething,' she replied huskily. 'I think perhaps
I'd better stay with him today . . .' She didn't look up
at Raoul.

'We'll both stay with him,' he surprised her by
saying. 'Or rather we'll take him with us. Don't forget
you'll need to equip a nursery for him before we leave
Paris, and we've only got a couple more days.'

He bent down, one lean finger touching Saud's hot

cheek, his knuckles accidentally grazing her breast. Her response was instant and electrifying, awareness flooding her body. All Raoul's attention focused on her as he studied her flushed cheeks, his eyes slowly dropping to her breasts and lingering there for several seconds. It took a considerable effort of will-power to keep her breathing steady and even; to busy herself with Saud as though she was completely unaware of the way Raoul was looking at her, or her body's immediate physical response to it.

'I'll get Saud dressed. If we're getting short of time we'd better not waste any of it.'

It was amazing that she managed to sound so calm, when her whole world had been jolted off its axis. No man had ever aroused such a reaction within her. If Raoul had leaned forward and stripped the nightdress from her body, she wouldn't have made the slightest move to stop him. And if he had touched the flesh where his glance had lingered . . . A wave of heat burned through her. What on earth was she thinking? She was glad that Raoul had turned away and had not witnessed that betraying tide of colour. Her reaction must have had something to do with the tenderness she had seen fleetingly in his eyes as he bent to touch Saud. Yes, that must be it! His affection for the little boy had caught her off guard.

Feeling relieved that she had managed to find an explanation for her unusual reaction, Claire waited until the door had closed firmly behind him before moving from the bed. A glimpse of her own reflection in one of the room's many mirrors arrested her, fresh colour storming her cheeks as she realised how transparent the fine cotton actually was, every line of her body revealed through it. What was she worrying about? Raoul was hardly likely to be aroused by the sight of her naked form. Hadn't he already told her how much he despised her? And he was hardly likely to be short of admiring female companionship.

For some reason the thought was a depressing one, but Claire didn't pause to analyse why. She was growing adept at avoiding unpleasant issues, she recognised wryly, as she bathed and dressed Saud, forcing her mind to turn to Raoul's plans for the remainder of the day.

CHAPTER FOUR

THEIR shopping spree finished, the purpose of their presence in Paris achieved, Claire found her thoughts turning again and again to the country which was to be her home for the next twelve to eighteen months. Rather than ask Raoul about his country, she had secretly managed to buy some books about the Middle East from a book store selling books in both French and English and she pored over these, alone in her room after Saud was asleep.

Omarah, it seemed, was one of the most forward-thinking of the Gulf States and reputedly one of the most beautiful, with a long coastline along the Persian Gulf and a wild hinterland behind it where the nomadic life of its desert inhabitants was preserved and protected. Careful forward-thinking had resulted in a diversification of business interests. Omarah was the centre of the Middle Eastern banking world, with a university that prided itself on the number and excellence of its science graduates, and technological progress had been carefully matched by a retention of Muslim values and the tolerance on which all Muslim races prided themselves towards adherents of other religions. Unlike many of the other Gulf States, Omarah possessed a capital that had its roots in antiquity. That Belthar had been a port of renown when Baghdad was still a village was a common boast, or so Claire read, and her senses were stirred by the photographs in her guide book, depicting, as they did, scenes she felt could not be rivalled by Hollywood's most lavish Arabian Nights fantasies.

On the last night of their stay in Paris, Raoul surprised her by announcing they would dine in the hotel's most exclusive restaurant. Claire wanted to refuse, but Raoul coolly overrode her objections.

Among the clothes he had bought for her was a Dior model lavishly designed; a swathe of off-white satin covering her from throat to ankle at the front, but dipping down to her waist at the back. The fabric enhanced her pale colouring, drawing attention to the size and depth of her eyes. With it Claire wore the diamond and emerald earrings Raoul had bought for her, the diamonds throwing out tongues of fire when she studied her reflection in her mirror. The slender sheath of silk made her look taller and somehow fragile, her hair a silver veil curving down on to her shoulders. She was just slipping into high-heeled sandals when she heard the knock on her door. Expecting the maid who was to watch over Saud, she called out 'Come in,' sudden tension infusing her muscles as the door opened and Raoul walked in.

Dressed in formal evening clothes, he projected a devastating image of male beauty; the same sort of beauty possessed by a mountain leopard, Claire thought, shuddering slightly; a beauty that engendered fear and gave birth to a curling sensation of pain cramping through her lower stomach. He studied her without comment, and she had to bite back the childish desire to demand if he was satisfied with what he saw. Everything she was wearing he had paid for, and as he watched her she felt a bitter impulse to tear

off the silk dress and the fine underwear she was
wearing beneath it and to fling them at his feet,
together with the priceless gems adorning her ears,
and to tell him she would rather go naked through the
streets then wear clothes paid for with his money. But
she quelled the impulse, telling herself she was being
stupid. Like herself, he was simply a pawn in a very
dangerous and difficult game. There could be no
personal relationship between them, they were simply
actors, each playing a part.

The feeling that she had somehow strayed into an
extravagant play was accentuated when they walked
into the restaurant. For a moment, Claire was dazzled
by the sophistication of the other diners. Women
glittered with expensive jewels, their bodies wrapped
in *haute couture* gowns. Conversation rose and fell in
dizzying waves and although she was loath to confess
it, Claire was glad of the elegant length of Raoul's
body alongside her own. Dangerous and lethal as a
black cheetah he might be, engendering fear and
awareness in every part of her body, but he was also a
protection against the battery of curious eyes studying
her, observing their progress across the room.

'Raoul!'

Claire came out of her panic-stricken reverie to
register the scrape of a chair being thrust back and the
husky, vaguely familiar masculine voice exclaiming
Raoul's name as its occupant got to his feet. Only
slightly less tall than Raoul, the resemblance between
them was so marked that Claire knew without even
considering the matter that she was looking at Raoul's
father. His companion had also got to her feet. She
was young, about her own age, but Claire barely had

time to register the avid look of appreciation in curious brown eyes before Raoul's father was reaching out to embrace her, not casually as he might have embraced an acquaintance, but intimately as befitted a true daughter-in-law.

'I read that you were in Paris, and that you were married. If I read the papers aright, you have made me a grandfather.' Speculative grey eyes rested thoughtfully on Claire's flushed face. 'Forgive me if I seem surprised, *mon cher*, but somehow from what I had read I expected your bride to appear much less . . . innocent.'

Something flashed briefly in Raoul's eyes, whether anger or contempt Claire could not be sure, and for a second she held her breath, wondering if he would look at her again, and see in her face what his father had.

'It seems your sins have caught you out, my son,' the Frenchman was continuing. 'Ahmed always was strongly morally motivated . . .'

'A fact of which you were undoubtedly aware when you seduced my mother and implanted her with your seed,' Raoul grated back. 'I hope you are praying to Allah that Ahmed might be granted a long life, Father, for once he is dead you need not look to me to continue the generous allowance he permits you.' His mouth curled contemptuously as he looked past Claire to the brunette standing by his father's side. 'How will you pay for your little diversions then, I wonder?'

'How easy it is for you to condemn. But then you have never gone hungry, never felt the gnawing ache that springs from poverty. You are more my son than you will ever allow yourself to admit. There was only one woman who mattered to me. Your mother knew that. I was always honest with her on that score. My little Marie was killed, killed by the Germans just before Paris was liberated. Your mother knew of my love for Marie. I made her no excuses for what I was, no apologies for loving Marie more than I loved her. Your mother was a spoiled child, Raoul, and I was lonely and bitter enough to think that what she could give me might be some sort of compensation. One day you will love a woman as I loved Marie, and then you will understand.'

When he had finished speaking there was silence. Claire had expected to dislike him, but instead she felt moved to a reluctant pity. She glanced into Raoul's face, shocked by the bitter contempt she saw there.

'I might feel more charitable about your denial of my mother, and of myself, if it were not for the fact that you have lived off us both for so many years.'

'No, you hate me because I couldn't love you as a man should love his son,' his father said calmly. 'I cannot lie to you, Raoul, nor put right an old wrong. From the moment of your birth you were your mother's son, a child of her heritage. I confess I was surprised when I read that Ahmed had compelled you into this marriage for the sake of the child you had conceived. Knowing you as I do, I thought you would rather have cut off your right arm than deny yourself to your own child, especially a son, but then perhaps there is more of me in you than you wish to admit.'

Raoul's face was bone-white with fury, his eyes glittering almost black in the mask of bone and skin, and Claire reacted instinctively, speaking almost without thinking as she sought to defuse the situation.

'Raoul didn't know about ... about the baby,' she interceded huskily. 'We quarrelled and I didn't tell him ...'

'But somehow Ahmed found out, and now you are married? She is very loyal to you, this wife of yours, Raoul, more loyal than your mother ever was to me. She couldn't wait to run home to her family to complain that I didn't love her as she believed I ought, even though I had told her what our marriage would be.'

'Lucien ...' The brunette pouted, bored with a conversation which excluded her, and Claire shrank from the contempt in Raoul's eyes as they moved from his father to the pouting girl at his side.

'You insult the memory of my mother to speak her name in the company of such a ... *putain* as this, and if you were not my father ...'

'You would what? Have me stoned to death? There is little of the Frenchman in you, is there, my son? Take care that fierce pride of yours does not blind you to what you really want from life. You are very like your mother. Had she listened properly to what I told her, our life together could have been a comfortable one ...'

'With both of you living on her wealth?'

'We made a bargain, she and I. Which is the greater dishonour I wonder? To renege on one's word or to live off one's wife?' With a sudden switch of mood that startled her, Raoul's father turned to Claire and said courteously, 'When you have finished dining perhaps you will allow me to dance with you, always supposing, of course, that my son permits?'

'I ...'

'We are newly-married, *mon père*. Tonight Claire will be in no one's arms but mine.'

Raoul's fingers on her arm urged her forward before his father could add anything further, and although he seemed to be completely in control of himself, Claire was painfully aware of the biting grip he had on her arm and knew that in the morning her skin would bare bruises from his touch.

The altercation with his father had taken away what little appetite she had had, and she shivered as she tried to study the menu, stunned when Raoul took it away from her.

'I am not hungry and neither, I suspect, are you,' he said abruptly, 'we will dance and perhaps our appetites will return.' He made no other reference to his father, and Claire was reluctant to bring the subject up. Neither did she particularly want to dance with him, but she sensed that to refuse him would be like a torch applied to dry tinder, igniting the temper she could sense he was struggling to control.

He was an excellent dancer, but she was too acutely conscious of the proximity of his body to hers to relax completely. The top of her head barely reached his shoulder and she was strongly aware of the warm, musky scent of his body, of the tautly controlled anger he was banking down. He bent his head and she had a momentary glimpse of something approaching deep pain in his eyes, before he banished it. Her heart ached with a tender pity and an insane desire to comfort him.

Was she completely mad? It would be like trying to comfort a wounded cheetah, and she would be mauled agonisingly in the process. His experiences with his parents had left him emotionally scarred and defensive, so much so that she doubted that any human being could get really close to him, and those foolish enough to try would receive the full force of his raging anger.

Across the room Claire's eyes instinctively searched for Lucien D'Albro. Did he realise how severely his rejection had damaged his son?

'What's the matter? Wishing you were with my father?' The bitter savagery of his taunt caught Claire completely unawares. 'I know you were speaking about him,' Raoul continued before she could speak. 'He has the reputation for being a first-rate lover.'

'Unlike you,' Claire retorted scathingly, hating the way he was looking at her, with a cynicism that bordered on complete contempt. 'Making love with you would be like ... like being mauled by a ... a wild animal,' she flung at him without bothering to weigh her words, realising her danger only when his lips parted in a feral smile that froze the blood in her veins.

'I think we will finish this conversation in the privacy of our suite.' It was impossible for her to resist the pressure of his fingers curling round her arm as he practically dragged her bodily from the floor. Pride and pride alone kept her from crying out in protest as he propelled her into the foyer and towards the lifts.

By the time they got upstairs he would have got his temper back under control, he was furiously angry with her now but it wouldn't last. He didn't even desire her, Claire comforted herself as the lift bore them upwards and he retained his savage hold on her. In a thick silence he pushed her into their sitting-room. All the protests and objections she had prepared mentally died on her lips as he dragged her through the sitting-room and into his own bedroom, locking the door behind them. It was only when he pocketed the key that she realised the extent of her danger and how far she had underestimated his mood. Black, terrifying rage simmered in the depths of his eyes as he released her arm, and laughed mirthlessly as she fled to the locked door.

'Oh no, you won't escape that easily,' he taunted her. 'Downstairs you sympathised with my father, didn't you?'

'I always try to see both sides of a story,' Claire palliated.

She had hoped to soothe him, but fear raced through her as he smiled coldly, his voice chilling her skin as he said softly, 'Oh good, then you'll understand why I want you to fully appreciate my mother's. Tonight it seemed to me that you were distinctly unsympathetic towards her—a young girl, the wife of a man who neither loved nor respected her. By tomorrow you should be much closer to appreciating her position.'

He took off his jacket and started to unfasten the buttons of his shirt with a slow purposefulness that mesmerised her. 'Of course, she was an innocent virgin, while you are a woman of the world, but then by all accounts my father is a far more considerate and appreciative lover than I. What was it you said . . . it would be like making love with a wild animal? I shall try not to disappoint you.'

This couldn't be happening to her, Claire thought wildly, closing her eyes to blot out the terrifying image of Raoul slowly and deliberately removing his shirt, his eyes pinpoints of black ice in the taut sleekness of his face. Her fingers tugged ineffectually at the locked door, panic stirring deep inside her, threatening to overwhelm her, in a primitive and helpless bid for flight. She wouldn't add to the futility of what was happening by running from him like a terrified animal trying to escape the talons of its captor. She would try to retain the remnants of her self-control, to . . .

A small sob escaped her as she felt ungentle hands on her shoulders, quickly turning her, seeking the fastening of her gown and sliding it from her shoulders. As Raoul turned her to face him, she crossed her hands over her exposed breasts instinctively, her eyes opening wide as she heard Raoul's acid exclamation, overriding her small cries of protest as he pried her protective fingers away from her body, forcing her hands down to her sides as her gown slid in a silken heap to the floor and his gaze roamed boldly over her naked curves. No man had ever seen her like this, nor studied her so intimately, and a deep flush of shame seared her skin.

In the lamplit room, Raoul's skin gleamed soft bronze, a tangle of dark hairs revealed by his open shirt. His flesh so dark in contrast to hers transfixed her gaze, her mouth suddenly so dry that she had to touch her tongue to her lips to moisten their contours. Dark eyes followed the intimate gesture, the fingers which had been clamping her arm to her side moving slowly over her body, stroking the curve of her hip which the brevity of her silk briefs did nothing to conceal. Tremors of reaction coursed through her body, the silken intimacy of Raoul's fingers against it triggering off strange waves of sensation. The soft pink areolae of her nipples seemed to swell and harden, and cool brown fingers were leaving the curve of her waist to investigate the rosy peaks.

'How very responsive you are, an enticement any man would find hard to ignore.' Without her being aware of it, Raoul had moved closer to her. His tongue brushed the soft outline of her lips, her eyes widening in astonishment as her body registered its response to his light touch. His tongue moved over her mouth again and Claire found her lips parting, wanting against her will a deeper contact. Her near nudity was forgotten as Raoul's mouth moved lightly against her own, teasing and tormenting until without being aware of it she was moving closer to him, like a moth attracted to the flame; realising too late, when she was helpless, held fast in his arms, his mouth plundering the innocence of hers with a bruising pressure that shocked and frightened her, what she had done.

Her breasts were crushed against the hard wall of his chest, his mouth enforcing his dominance over her, his fingers tightening on her hip bones as he moulded her against his body.

'Raoul, please don't do this,' she begged in a panicky voice when his mouth finally released hers. Her lips felt swollen and bruised, her voice unfamiliar even to her own ears, edged with fear and hysteria.

'Pleading with me, Claire? You should know better than to plead with a wild animal.' His voice possessed a hypnotic quality that held a deadly fascination, and despite the warmth of his room Claire shivered, gasping in shock and outrage when his hand spread possessively against her breast. His thumb stroked slowly over her nipple and the dark head bent. Fierce shafts of pleasure seemed to jolt through her body, a crazy, mindless frenzy taking possession of her. 'Claire . . .'

The shrill command of the telephone cut through the heavy silence, and Raoul released her almost instantly to go and answer it. He spoke into the receiver in Arabic, frowning as he turned and saw her, her gown still on the floor, her arms wrapped round her body. Murmuring something curtly into the receiver, he put it down and came towards her, taking the door key out of his pocket.

'Saved this time from the mauling of the wild animal.' The anger had gone completely from his expression. 'Is that relief or disappointment I see in your eyes, Claire?' he added mockingly as she edged away from him. 'Your body is quite intoxicatingly responsive. Your lovers must have taught you well . . . or is it simply frustration that made you so hungry in my arms?'

He picked up the receiver before she could retaliate and tell him that she had felt nothing in his embrace apart from fear and loathing. He had treated her as though she were a rag doll incapable of feelings and her pride was as bruised as her mouth. He was an animal, a dangerous animal she would be wise not to tangle with again if she valued her self-respect and her safety. She had always sworn that when she did share the pleasure of intimacy with a man, it would be with a man she respected and trusted as well as loved, and yet she was forced to admit that she had come dangerously close to forgetting all the tenets by which she had previously lived her life when Raoul held her in his arms. Those light teasing kisses had inflamed her to the point where nothing else had mattered other than the hard possession of his mouth, and without the brutality of the kiss he had forced upon her she doubted that she would have been able to break free of the spell he seemed to have woven round her senses.

Safe in her own room she dismissed the maid and then locked the door behind her, telling herself that it was just as well she had found out what manner of man lurked behind the urbane exterior Raoul showed to the world. Now there would be no danger of her falling prey to his potent maleness. But as she lay on the verge of sleep she was forced to admit that there had been excitement as well as fear in her reaction to him; that her body had responded overwhelmingly to his touch and that she would have to keep a stricter guard over her emotions.

'Welcome to Omarah!'

They had flown Concorde to Omarah in less than half the time it would have taken on a normal flight, and Claire inclined her head slightly towards Raoul as she followed him down the gangway, her body trying to adjust itself to the intense heat of the Gulf afternoon. Heat lay in a haze of dust over the city beyond the modern airport; minarets and mosaics vying with skyscrapers, the mingling of East and West an assault on Claire's senses as she tried to assimilate the contrasting cultures.

A Mercedes limousine was waiting to ferry them from the airport to what was to be Claire's home for the duration of their stay. She knew that Muslim families lived together, and had somehow expected that she would be sharing the woman's quarters of someone else's home but Raoul announced, as their driver negotiated the narrow streets of the souk, and then open, gracious boulevards, that the Sheikh had put one of his palaces at their disposal. 'It is on the gulf, away from the city. The air is more healthy there for Saud.'

It was disconcerting to learn that they would be living alone together. When she had visualised her life in Omarah Claire had envisioned a life shared in the main with other women, rather than with Raoul who she had imagined would have as little desire for her company as she had for his, but her doubts and fears were forgotten as the city was left behind and they took the coast road along the gulf, past sugar-icing places, Moorish in concept, decorated with iron grilles.

They had gone several miles before they turned off the main road and bumped down a narrow track which came to a full stop in front of a pale pink palace, its narrow slit windows staring haughtily in the direction they had just travelled. As though by some magic signal, two doors opened in the high wall surrounding the palace and the Mercedes purred silently inside.

They were in a courtyard enclosed by the high wall on one side and a row of what seemed to be garages and outhouses on the other. In the distance, Claire could hear the sound of water, and the brilliant sunshine cast harsh shadows over the coloured pavings. More utilitarian than decorative, the courtyard was faintly disappointing. She had expected something more exotic.

Raoul was climbing out of the car and coming round to open her door for her, a courtesy she hadn't expected, bearing in mind the much-publicised

superiority of the Middle Eastern male. The heat of
the afternoon struck her like a blow after the air-
conditioning of the car, and a wave of faintness swept
over her. Her body shrank from even the most
accidental contact with Raoul's, her eyes darkening as
she remembered the savagery of his assault on her
body. If the phone hadn't rung when it had . . .

She shivered suddenly, forcing down her fear. If
Raoul had been savage it was because he had been
angry. Meeting his father had opened old wounds and
he had reacted instinctively, wanting to hit out and
hurt as he had been hurt.

'Are you all right?' He asked the question
automatically and Claire nodded her head.

'Just tired, that's all.' She leaned into the car to take
Saud, as always finding comfort and strength in
holding the child. A link had been forged between
them the day she had saved Saud from death, and in
some strange way it was almost as though he *were* her
child.

A door opened in the palace wall, and taking a deep
breath Claire followed Raoul towards it. She was now
in his country, and would be judged as his wife; the
woman who had borne his child outside marriage and
who he had been forced to marry by his uncle. For
Saud's sake she must play her part perfectly. Head
held high, Claire followed him into the cavernous
darkness waiting beyond the open door.

CHAPTER FIVE

'If the Sitt would come with me.'

As her eyes accustomed themselves to the darkness, Claire saw that she was being addressed by a girl in her late teens. Pretty and slender, her dark eyes regarded Claire rather anxiously, but her smile was warmly welcoming, and Claire was too tired to do anything other than follow her up what seemed to be an everlasting spiral of stone stairs, narrow slit windows giving her the occasional glimpse of sea and land spread out below them. By the time they reached the top, Saud had become a heavy weight in her arms, but mindful of the real reason for her presence here in this palace which made her feel totally alien, she was reluctant to let him go.

At last they stopped climbing and her companion indicated an arched doorway decorated with a fretted frieze of stylised flowers and symbols. Claire already knew that it was forbidden for a Muslim to copy directly from nature, but the intricacy of the detail of the frieze had a beauty all of its own. The heavy wooden door slid open under her companion's touch, and at first Claire was almost blinded by the brilliance of the sunset flooding the enormous room. Tall arched windows looked out across the gulf, the scent of sandalwood hung evocatively on the evening air. A large low bed on a raised dais caught her attention, its gauzy hangings moving lightly in the air-conditioning.

Brilliantly hued silk and satin cushions were heaped on the bed and on the divan just below the windows.

It had been decided when Claire accepted the Sheikh's proposition that she would have almost sole care of Saud. 'It will not be thought of as unusual since you are a European,' the Sheikh had told her, 'and it will make the task of guarding him much simpler.'

After her companion had introduced herself as Zenaide, and had explained that she was to be her personal maid, she turned to the wall opposite the windows and opened a door set into it indicating that Claire was to follow her.

A narrow corridor lined on one side with floor-to-ceiling wardrobes opened out into a small square room with three doors off it. One of them led into a sumptuous bathroom, the huge sunken bath in the middle of the room making Claire draw a rather shaky breath. Two people could easily fit inside it, and hard on the heels of that thought came a vivid and tormenting mental image of Raoul, naked, his tawny skin gleaming with water as a dark-eyed, doe-like houri bathed his body.

More disturbed than she wanted to admit, Claire hurried out of the bathroom, heaving a faint sigh of relief as Zenaide opened one of the other doors and she realised that she was in Saud's room. Nearly as large as her own it was rather bare, apart from a cot and a highchair, but once the furniture they had chosen in Paris arrived it would look much more cheerful. She would have liked to suggest having a mural painted on the walls—woodland creatures, scenes from *Jungle Book* and *Winnie the Pooh*, but guessed that it would not be permitted. Saud was, after all, a Muslim child, but perhaps once she had got to know Zenaide a little better she could discover from the girl how they could make the room look more attractive and stimulating for the baby.

When they emerged once more into the small, square ante-room, Claire glanced curiously at the third door, but Zenaide made no move to open it, and when Claire asked her what lay behind it she blushed a little and murmured, 'It is the room of the Lord Raoul. Once many years ago this was the suite of the Sultan's favourite woman but Sheikh Ahmed has given instructions that this suite was to be prepared for the Lord Raoul and the Sitt.'

From Zenaide's stumbling explanation and obvious embarrassment Claire divined that it was not the custom for married couples to live so closely together, and indeed her reading had given her to believe that she and Raoul would live completely separate lives. For a moment a *frisson* of fear touched against her spine as she remembered Raoul's bitter passion in Paris, but she banished it quickly, reminding herself that on that occasion he had been under severe provocation and that now it was necessary if they were to protect Saud properly for them to have as much privacy as possible. Indeed, it was comforting to know that Saud's room could only be reached through her own or Raoul's.

Shifting the sleeping weight of the little boy on to her other arm, she followed Zenaide back to her own room. What did the Arab girl think about her and her marriage? Was she shocked that the 'Lord Raoul', as she called him, had married a European girl, or was it

already common knowledge in Omarah that the
Sheikh had compelled Raoul to marry her for the sake
of 'their' child? Zenaide struck her as a kind, gentle
girl, and perhaps once they had got to know one
another better they might be able to talk as friends.

'If you will allow me to take the Lord Saud,'
Zenaide began when they were back in Claire's room.

'No. No, it's all right, I prefer to look after him
myself,' Claire told her, robbing the words of any
unkindness with a warm smile. 'He's not really used to
strangers yet.'

'You are lucky to be able to care for him yourself,'
Zenaide told her. 'My own sister, who is married to a
second cousin of the Sheikh, has three sons, but their
nursemaid will not allow her to care for them. Poor
Yasmin would like to dismiss her, but if she does the
girl's family could starve. The Sheikh is trying to
educate all our people so that all can find work, but it
is not always easy.'

It couldn't be, Claire agreed mentally. Superstition
and custom were always barriers to education. People
treated change with suspicion and fear, clinging on to
what was familiar. As she glanced out of the window
and saw the waters of the gulf dyed crimson by the
setting sun, she shivered briefly, startled by the
unfamiliar and mournful sound of the muezzin, and
watched as Zenaide gracefully obeyed the summons of
her religion. As an instinctive mark of respect she too
remained still and silent until the eerie sound had died
away and Zenaide was on her feet once more.

While Claire bathed and fed Saud, Zenaide
unpacked her cases, openly admiring the things Raoul
had bought her in Paris. One of the new silk

nightgowns was carefully laid out on the large bed, and watching Zenaide's hennaed hands gently smoothing the fragile fabric, Claire wondered what Zenaide really thought about her—a woman who had borne a child out of wedlock and who, because of that child, had been forced to come here to a strange land and live among a race who prized female virtue above all things.

When Raoul did eventually marry, what manner of woman would he choose? Not a European, she thought immediately. No, he would choose a girl like Zenaide, innocent and obedient; a girl who would worship him from afar, grateful for whatever crumbs of affection he gave her. Had he ever been in love? He had mentioned an arranged marriage to her, had he loved her, a girl forbidden to him because of their differing religions?

A tap on the outer door startled her, and Zenaide went to open it, a pretty jewelled moth in her floor-length caftan with its glittering embroidery. A man stood outside, tall and robed. He murmured something to Zenaide in Arabic, his teeth white in his tanned, bearded face.

'That is Ali, the Lord Raoul's body-servant. The Lord Raoul has sent him to tell you that it is time to eat. Ali will escort you.'

Time to eat? Claire glanced helplessly at her creased suit. She had been so busy with Saud that she hadn't even had time to wash her hands and face, never mind change her clothes. And who was she supposed to eat with? Raoul? Surely she had read that in the East men and women ate separately, men first and then the women afterwards?

Guessing from Zenaide's anxious expression that it would be a mark of disrespect to keep Ali waiting, Claire hurried to the door, puzzled to see that Ali averted his face from her as she did so, until she remembered that it was forbidden by the Prophet for a man to look into the face of a wife of another, and that this was the reason women wore the all-covering burnous.

Ali led her back down the stairs she had come up with Zenaide, pausing after three flights to indicate the door which lay beyond the small hallway with its rich Persian carpet and decorative wall-hanging.

The room beyond the door looked out over the sea like her own, but darkness had fallen with the swiftness of a deep blue velvet cloak studded with diamanté during her short journey down the stairs and the room was illuminated with the soft glow of many lamps, secured on the walls.

At first as the door closed behind her Claire thought she was alone in the vast chamber. A divan ran the length of the window, heaped with silk cushions, three other divans were arranged close to the long low table in the centre of the room. Priceless silk rugs adorned the floor, the smell of sandalwood once more tantalised her.

'If you would care to sit down, I shall instruct Ali to serve our meal.'

Raoul's voice reaching her from the shadows startled her and she swung round, her eyes widening as he came towards her. Gone was the urbane, dark-suited businessman and in his place was a stranger dressed in a soft white robe, moving as silent and sure-footed as a mountain lion as he came towards her, cynicism curving a deep line on either side of his mouth as he observed her astonishment.

'When in Rome do as the Romans do, is that not a familiar saying to you? We of the East have learned that it is easier to do business with the West when we accept its mode of dress, but you will not see many men wearing pin-striped suits walking the streets of Omarah.'

More than ever Claire wished that she had had the opportunity to wash and change. Compared with Raoul, she felt grubby and travel-worn and she wondered if he had arranged matters deliberately so that she would feel at a disadvantage.

'Should we be eating alone together like this?' she challenged, wanting him to know that she wasn't completely ignorant of his country's customs.

'It is known that you are not of the Muslim religion or of our country and allowances will be made. Besides there are matters we still have to discuss. Please sit down.'

She did so awkwardly, trying to tuck her legs beneath her as she subsided on to one of the divans and watched as Ali opened the door and their meal was brought in. Saffron rice, and other delicacies Claire could not recognise were placed before them, Ali watching hawk-eyed to make sure that everything was in order. When the food was set out and the servants had withdrawn, Ali also left the room, closing the door behind him. Raoul, who had been standing by the window, came and sat down on the divan opposite her, his supple body easily accommodating itself to the narrow, low furniture, increasing Claire's awareness of the awkwardness of her own limbs.

'What are you waiting for?' Raoul drawled when Claire continued to sit without moving. 'Or is it that you fear our food will be offensive to your westernised palate?'

He was mocking her, Claire suspected, because the saffron rice and sweet-smelling lamb both looked delicious. 'I thought it was the custom for the man to eat first,' she reponded calmly. Raoul's eyebrows rose.

'Yes, at a formal banquet, or in an old-fashioned household; indeed in times gone by a man might feed his falcon before he fed his favourite houri, but I have no intention of starving you, Claire. My uncle has given us this palace as our home because it is relatively easy to guard,' he continued, changing the subject. 'As you will have observed it faces the sea and is protected on all other sides by its own wall. It was once the stronghold of what in Europe would have been called a pirate. Those rooms you share with Saud have in their time housed many a stolen European beauty destined for the Sultan's bed.' He laughed harshly when Claire shuddered. 'Times change, and now there is no need for us to use force to compel Western women into our beds; they are only too anxious to be there, and so have lost much of their value.'

'I can't believe that all Muslim women are as pure as the driven snow,' Claire countered, impelled to defend her fellow European women.

'Perhaps not, but they are the product of centuries of women who know how to please a man and make it their life's work to do so. You are happy with your rooms?' he asked once again changing the subject.

'They have been very well chosen,' Claire agreed.

'The only way anyone could get into Saud's room is through mine, or . . .'

'Mine? Yes. I am sure that no one suspects the truth, but it is always wise to take every precaution. While you are living here as my wife a certain standard of behaviour will be expected of you. Ramadan is behind us now and you may expect to receive bride visits from the female members of my uncle's family. Zenaide will help you if there is any point on which you are in doubt.'

'And you? Will you be . . .?'

'Will I be what?' Raoul taunted. 'At your side like a duitiful caring husband? You have forgotten surely that this "marriage" has been forced upon me for the sake of "our" son. There are business matters which compel me to spend time in the city, but you need not fear, the palace will be guarded at all times.'

Why did she feel as though she was suddenly being deserted? Raoul meant nothing to her, and yet unbidden her fingers pressed lightly on her lips, as though she could still feel the pressure of his mouth on hers. It came to her then, on a jolting shock wave, that she *wanted* to feel his mouth against hers again and the food before her was forgotten as she stared blindly towards him, shaken by the discovery but knowing it was something she had held at bay from the first moment she saw him.

She had been attracted to him then although she had fought against admitting it, and when he had kissed her there had been part of her that revelled in the hard, bruising contact of his mouth on hers, that yearned for the touch of his fingers against her skin.

'Is something wrong?' The green eyes narrowed,

skimming her too-pale face. Another second and he would surely guess the truth, Claire thought in panic.

'No ... no. I'm just tired ... I should like to go back to my room.'

Raoul inclined his head. 'If you wish. I shall have Ali escort you there. Tomorrow I must go to the palace. My uncle will have returned and we have much to discuss.'

Back in her own room Claire discovered that she was in truth tired. Zenaide was waiting for her, and despite her protests, insisted on helping her to undress and on bathing her. How different it would be if it was Raoul who was with her, caressing her perfumed skin while she caressed him. Clamping down on the feverish intensity of her thoughts, Claire dismissed Zenaide, assuring the concerned girl that she was quite well, merely suffering a little from jet lag and exhaustion.

On her way back to her bedroom, she paused outside Saud's door, and pushed it open. He lay on his back fast asleep, breathing evenly. When the new cot arrived from Paris perhaps she would ask Raoul if he could sleep with her in her room. She had grown dangerously fond of the little boy and already was dreading the parting that must eventually come.

Just thinking about it made her want to bend down and lift him out of his cot. It was the sudden rush of air that warned her that she was no longer alone and she straightened immediately, protecting the cot with her baby, her eyes wide and frightened in her pale face, the exposed skin of her shoulders and arms suddenly chilled by the air-conditioning. On dismissing Zenaide she had simply wrapped one of the large, plush towels around herself sarong-wise, but now she felt acutely vulnerable, her eyes searching the darkness beyond the open door as they sought the intruder.

'Claire!'

She sagged in relief on recognising Raoul's voice. 'Raoul, you frightened me.'

He came further into the room, a rather puzzling expression on his face, and Claire realised that although she had not at first been able to see him, he had quite clearly seen her in the glow of the lamp above Saud's bed.

'Yes, and yet your first instinct was to protect Saud.'

'An automatic reaction,' Claire told him shakily, not wanting to admit to the powerful love she had felt for the little boy ever since she saved his life. 'A piece of universal female programming.' As his eyes swept slowly over the cot and then shifted to her body she became acutely aware of how little she was wearing.

'You are cold?' Raoul frowned, his fingertips brushing the goose-bumps on her arms, 'or is it something else that causes your skin to react like this?'

Danger signals flashed from her body to her brain as his fingers became caressing, smoothing over her skin.

'I . . . I don't know what you mean.' How husky and uncertain her voice sounded, as well it might. She knew exactly what he meant and his smile told her that he knew it too.

'I mean desire, Claire,' he told her softly, 'and why should you not feel it? You are a woman used to the caresses of a man. I knew that in Paris. Your response was not that of a woman who is still unawakened.'

His fingers had reached her shoulder now and were

caressing the smooth roundness of her bones, somehow propelling her closer to him. Her nostrils were full of the clean warm male scent of him mingling with the wool of his robe.

'Raoul, please stop this,' she protested achingly. 'You do not desire me, you told me that . . .'

'I did not,' he corrected, 'but hunger has a way of stifling our more fastidious mental urgings, and all I know now is that my body is aroused by the cool paleness of yours, just as yours yearns for the possession of mine.'

'No!' She croaked the denial between stiff lips, horrified by the weakness invading her body. How could she still feel this way about him when with her own ears she had heard him callously describe how he felt about her? He still despised her, that hadn't changed, but now his body wanted her. As hers wanted him, she acknowledged inwardly, but it wasn't simply his physical possession she wanted. She wanted more.

For a split second it seemed as though her heart had stopped beating. A panicky, suffocating sensation washed over her. No, no, it couldn't be true. She wasn't in love with him! She started to tremble, gasping aloud as she felt the warm abrasiveness of Raoul's robe pressed against her skin. His arms were round her, holding her against him, letting her know that he hadn't lied when he said she aroused him. She could feel the heat coming off his skin, the fierce compulsive pressure of his thighs and the unmistakable hardness of his body against hers.

His hands tugged at her towel, urging it away from her body, his mouth exploring the vulnerable curve of her throat, his tongue brushing delicately against her ear until she was mindless with hazy pleasure, her arms around his neck, her fingers luxuriating in the feel of his thick dark hair. The golden glow from the lamp bathed her body, but she was no longer conscious of her nudity, only of Raoul's hands moving across it, travelling the length of her spine. He murmured huskily as she arched instinctively against him, the fierce throb of his body pounding out a siren song she was unable to resist, and which echoed in the heated rhythm of the blood coursing through her body. Her throat arched in mute pleasure beneath the warm exploration of Raoul's mouth, capturing and feeding the frantic pulse beating there until she could hear the blood roaring in her ears, and her body felt as supple and as pliable as a length of silk.

'Claire.' He murmured her name against her lips as his tongue teased their moist curves; her fingers were trembling as they investigated the opening of his robe, following the shape of his shoulders, lost in a daze of mute pleasure. She had never dreamed that the mere touch of skin beneath her fingers could convey such a kaleidoscope of delight. Raoul's mouth brushed against her own, and finding it softly closed, hardened demandingly, his teeth nipping at her bottom lip, his tongue stroking persuasively against it until her mouth opened and fierce sparks of pleasure shot through her body as his tongue slid moistly against hers, exploring and enticing, until she was moaning softly into his mouth, half delirious with the pleasure he was giving her.

The reason she was in his arms was forgotten, her body offering its own incitement as it arched and

stroked against him. The low groan that came from
deep in his throat as his hands swept upwards towards
her breasts offered further excitement, her body
abandoned in its response to the desire she could feel
building in his. Once again Claire felt her breasts swell
and harden beneath his touch, but this time it wasn't
just the hard pad of his thumb that brushed her
sensitive flesh. His mouth lifting from hers, Raoul
bent his head, the lamplight revealing to her the dark
flush staining his cheekbones and the feverish glitter
in his eyes. His tongue touched her breasts lightly,
almost exploratively, but Claire could feel the build up
of tension in his body which ignited the smouldering
fires already burning in her own.

With almost feverish intensity she pressed herself
against him, her fingers curling into the dark hair
covering his chest, her lips raining tiny, hungry kisses
against his throat, her whole body convulsing with
fierce pleasure as she felt the cool breath he expelled
against her breast and almost simultaneously the
shudder that racked his body, his mouth opening over
her taut nipple.

A shiver of ecstasy surged over her, her small white
teeth biting into the tanned smoothness of his skin, as
she sought to communicate the need building up
inside her. He tasted faintly of salt, the musky scent of
his body increased her arousal. When his hand slid
down to her thigh she welcomed his touch, every
nerve-ending in her body urging her on towards
fulfilment.

Somewhere in the distance she was dimly aware of a
sound trying to penetrate the fog of desire blanketing
her. Gradually the sound became louder, and she

recognised it as Saud's crying. In the same moment as she tensed, Raoul released her and she dropped back to earth with a humiliating thump, hastily reaching for her discarded towel and wrapping it quickly round her body before turning towards Saud.

Her thoughts a jumble of confused impressions and fears, she reached automatically for the crying child, barely noticing that Raoul had gone until she turned round. It took her fifteen minutes to soothe Saud whose teeth were still troubling him, and by the time he was asleep all she could think of was how much she hoped she never had to set eyes on Raoul again as long as she lived.

What must he think of her? Her face stung with scarlet colour. She knew what he thought of her. He thought her an experienced woman of the world who thought nothing of satisfying her physical need with whatever man happened to be handy. But if they had continued to make love, he would have discovered for himself that she had had no previous lover.

She started to tremble, and as she hurried to her own room she tried to convince herself that it wasn't disappointment that made her limbs feel as weak as water and her pulses thud with a pagan need. What was the matter with her? Was she honestly naive enough to believe that once Raoul discovered her innocence he would fall madly in love with her? That sort of scenario belonged to love stories, not real life. Somehow she had the lowering feeling that if Raoul knew the truth he would be at great pains to avoid her. All he wanted was simply to assuage his own physical need and she had happened to be there.

And yet she couldn't help thinking about what

would have happened if Saud hadn't cried; if Raoul had taken her to the privacy of his own room, his body as naked as hers against the silk covers. She shivered suddenly in the darkness, perspiration springing up on her skin, a dull ache she refused to give a name to pulsing through her lower body. If she was wise she would keep her distance from Raoul from now on. Now only *she* knew she loved him, but if he should ever make love to her and discover the truth he would know how she felt about him. How contemptuous he would be. He felt nothing for her, and nor would he ever do so. He had chosen to follow the ways of his mother's people, and if he ever loved it would be a doe-eyed slender girl like Zenaide, not a pale-skinned blonde who couldn't even sit on a divan without getting cramp.

'The Sitt has a visitor.' Zenaide came quickly into the room, excitement sparkling in her eyes. Raoul had been gone for two days, and much to her amazement Claire had not felt either bored or lonely. This morning she had taken Saud down on to the beach, much to Zenaide's disapproval, but the little boy had thoroughly enjoyed the experience, and as the small bay could only be reached from the palace, Claire judged it private enough for safety.

'A visitor? But I don't know anyone,' Claire commented before she remembered Raoul's comments about 'bride visitors'.

'It is the mother of the Sheikh,' Zenaide told her importantly, her eyes round as saucers. 'Ali has put her in the salon that looks out over the main courtyard.'

Claire had discovered in Raoul's absence that the

palace had several inner courtyards, the most beautiful of which was the main courtyard with its mosaic-tiled floor and tranquil fish pond. Overlooked by what had once been the women's quarters, the courtyard was a small peaceful oasis of escape from the burning heat of the sun. Peach and fig trees provided cool splashes of green, their leaves carefully sprayed daily by the gardeners. Gleaming carp swam leisurely beneath large lily pads and Claire often brought Saud down to the courtyard when it was too hot to take him to the beach, enjoying his pleasure in the swift movement of the fish through the calm waters.

There was only one person in the large, formal salon, wrapped in black from head to foot and half a head shorter than Claire herself, with dark, alert eyes searching her face as she stepped into the room.

'So, you are Raoul's wife and the mother of his son.' The dark fabric was withdrawn from her visitor's face and Claire found herself looking at one of the wisest and most serene human faces she had ever seen. All that there had been in the Sheikh's mother's life was written in her face, both good and bad, and Claire knew instinctively that here was no dutiful Muslim woman content to be a mere cipher in her family's life. She exuded an air of wisdom and great serenity. She had known great love in her life and great pain too, Claire sensed, as she returned her greeting. She had Saud in her arms, and had brought him down thinking that her unexpected guest would want to see him.

'And this is Raoul's child.' Before Claire could stop her she had lifted Saud out of her arms, studying him thoughtfully, an expression Claire couldn't read darkening her eyes. 'He has little of you in him,' she said at length, 'and much of my son. Raoul will not be pleased by this marriage my son has forced upon him. As a child he always swore that he was more of the East than the West. Had he been allowed free choice he would have married his second cousin. All that was required was that he should change his religion, but Raoul has always been proud—and stubborn.'

She smiled briefly, her teeth still white and even in the dark olive of her face. How old she was Claire could not tell, but she had a bone structure that was ageless, and must have been very beautiful in her youth. Raoul was like her, Claire realised with an aching pang, and like her he would age well. 'His father had made his mother promise that she would bring him up in the Christian religion. That was the price she had to pay for deserting her husband and Raoul has continued to pay it for her.'

'If Raoul hates his father and his French inheritance so much, why has he not become a Muslim?' Claire asked.

'Perhaps because he wants to be accepted for what he is. It is always hard for a child torn between two cultures. Zenobi, Raoul's mother, was accepted back into her father's home, but she was never allowed to forget her sin in marrying outside her own faith and race, and it is always hard for a child to come to terms with the apparent rejection of a parent, although in Lucien's case . . .'

'He told Raoul's mother that he did not love her before they married.'

'So you know about that? Lucien was working here when they met. I liked him, but it was obvious that Zenobi could not see beyond her besotted adoration of him. What man could resist such a gift—a rich, adoring bride?' She shrugged fatalistically. 'I have always thought Lucien more sinned against than sinning, and one day Raoul too will accept this. He has already proved that he is not totally opposed to all Westerners,' she added dryly, smiling when Claire flushed. If only she knew the truth! If anything Raoul destested her even more than he disliked his father.

'I am honoured that you have come to visit me, Princess,' Claire murmured, trying to get the conversation back on to more mundane lines.

'Not just to visit you,' the old lady said calmly. 'A hundred miles is a long way for a woman of my years to travel without a purpose. For a long time now I have been looking for someone to continue my work after I am gone. The women of my family have their own concerns and much less freedom than I in my time.'

She saw Claire's look of astonishment and chuckled. 'I was born in the desert. My people were nomads and I knew no home but the desert until I married my husband. My bride-price was the strip of desert where Omarah's oil-wells are now situated.' She chuckled again. 'Poor Khalid, there were times when he wished he had taken a tame dove to wife rather than the wild kestrel that he called me. I was not used to the formality of the Sheikh's palace. My life had been one of freedom. I was the only child of a prince of the desert and proud of my heritage. Many of my tribe still roam the desert and it is my self-appointed task to help them. What we know as civilisation encroaches further into their homeland with every year that passes, making it harder and harder for them to survive. They are offered pieces of land on which to build homes and settle down, but what nomad can ever live in one place for long and not pine for shifting sands beneath his feet? But civilisation does have its benefits—medical care, education—and it is these that I try to bring to the women of the desert. They accept me because I am one of them, and today I intend to drive out to a small oasis where I know they will be encamped. You seem to me to be a woman of spirit, Raoul's English wife, I should like you to come with me. Remember,' she added cryptically as she realigned her all-enveloping robe, 'nothing that is worth having is ever easily won. Now, do you come with me?'

'Yes . . . Yes, I would love to,' Claire assured her eagerly, 'but I shall have to take Saud with me.'

Once again she saw a strange look flit across the older woman's face. 'It is a foolish man who seeks to part the lioness from her cub,' was all she said, standing up and walking towards the door.

Zenaide was nowhere in sight, but Claire found her maid waiting for her in her bedroom, placidly straightening the silk cushions. 'I will come with the Sitt,' she pronounced firmly when Claire told her where she was going, calmly producing two enveloping hooded cloaks similar to the one the Princess had worn.

It was a three-hour journey to the oasis and Claire stared overtly at the black tents pitched beneath the shade of the palms. Small children played noisily in their shadow, and several men were grooming the pale cream Arab horses which Claire knew were among the nomads' most prized possessions. The moment the Princess's car stopped it was surrounded, both men and women abasing themselves before her as she stepped out. An old, gnarled man whose proud bearing proclaimed him the leader of the tribe came forward and escorted them to the largest of the tents. Inside it was far more luxurious than Claire had dreamed, hung with silk tapestries, priceless rugs adorning the floor. The leader of the tribe departed and almost at once the tent became full of chattering women, as inquisitive as magpies as they stared at Claire's pale hair and skin, laughter gleaming in dark eyes as they spoke to one another.

'They are saying that when you lie with Raoul it will be like the sand caressed by the shadow of night,' the Princess translated with a brief smile. Claire coloured hotly at the smile, her embarrassment provoking another wave of amusement. 'Now they are saying that your cheeks are as pink as those of a maiden before she knows a man and that no one would think you had borne Lord Raoul's child.'

Hennaed fingers stroked and caressed Saud's plump baby limbs, and the small boy bore the caresses stoically until he was returned to Claire's arms. A maidservant came in carrying a huge samovar while another produced delicate bowls for coffee. As guest of honour, the Princess was served first, Claire next. The coffee, although fragrant, was too strong for her taste, just as the sweetly sticky sweetmeats were too rich for her stomach, and she winced to see how many were pressed upon small Saud, but was reluctant to intervene and possibly cause offence.

'You are thinking that too much rich food will make him sick,' the Princess murmured astutely to her. 'It is difficult for us to explain to them that it is better to give their children fresh fruit, and we can only make progress very slowly. The Badu are a proud people, fiercely independent, and to shut them away in a reservation of the sort they have in America and Australia for their native people would be to offer them a slow, tortuous death. However, children must be educated if they are to fit into our modern world. They trust me and I do what I can. They like you, wife of Raoul, and it pleases me to think that when I am gone you will continue my work among them. You have much compassion, I think, and not just for your own.' She touched Saud's head as she spoke and Claire wondered how much those wise eyes had seen. Had she guessed the truth about Saud? If so, the Princess would keep her own counsel, Claire was sure of that.

It was late when they left the oasis, dusk falling swiftly on the heels of the flaming sunset, wrapping the landscape in darkness. Claire was still fascinated by the glittering intensity of the stars in the desert sky, and peered out of the car window at them, Saud a warm and heavy weight in her arms.

The place was bustling with activity as their car swept into the courtyard. An unfamiliar black Mercedes made Claire's heart thump. Raoul? Had he returned? Refusing her offers of hospitality, the Princess explained that she had an appointment in the city which she wished to keep. 'We will meet again, wife of Raoul, and until then I pray that Allah will watch over you.'

In silence Claire and Zenaide climbed the stairs to Claire's quarters. She was tired and hungry, but still alert enough to freeze when she heard the sound of footsteps coming down the stairs towards her, angry determined footsteps which she was sure could only belong to one person.

As Raoul turned turned the angle of the stairs, he saw them, a bitter oath splintering the silence and making Zenaide tremble as she clung to Claire's side.

'So there you are! What happened, did you have second thoughts?'

'Seconds thoughts?' Unable to comprehend what he was talking about, Claire stared up at him. He turned to Zenaide.

'I wish to see your mistress alone. Return to your quarters. Come with me,' he ordered Claire. 'I want to know exactly where you took Saud and why. Did you think to double-cross us? To claim a large reward for Saud's safety? Is that why you stole away from here with him this afternoon?'

CHAPTER SIX

'STOLE away?' Anger and astonishment battled inside her, anger suddenly getting the upper hand. 'I am not prepared to talk to you about your absurd suspicions on the stairs, Raoul,' she flung over her shoulder as she walked swiftly past him. 'I am not a servant to be berated on an open stairway.'

'No,' Raoul agreed ferociously. 'What I have to say to you is better said in private, and think yourself lucky if I content myself with mere words. What I would like to do . . .'

'Is what? Torture me? Murder me? And all because I accepted an invitation from your grandmother to accompany her on a visit to an oasis?' Triumph edged under her calm voice, but she turned away so that he wouldn't see it. All at once she wanted to punish him, wanted to humiliate and hurt him as he had hurt her with his accusations and lack of trust. 'Perhaps I shouldn't have taken Saud with me, but I thought he was safer with me than left alone, and I wasn't sure if it might be construed as an insult if I refused the Princess's invitation.'

'This is true? You have been out with Faika? But she takes no one on her trips to the desert.'

'She took me,' Claire told him defiantly, 'and you are perfectly at liberty to check with her. She is on her way back to the city at the moment. Of course, if you do check with her she will guess the truth, perhaps she might even think you have given me reason to flee from you, taking our "son" with me.'

'I—I owe you an apology.' He had his back to her, but Claire could see how hard it was for him to say the words. 'When I came back and found you both missing, my first thought was that somehow someone had discovered the truth, but when Ali told me that no one had been admitted to the palace I thought you must have left alone.'

'And knowing of my greed, of course you knew immediately what had happened?'

She watched in mute fascination as the dark tide of colour swept up over the back of his neck. Proud, the Princess had called him, and Claire could well appreciate how difficult he must be finding that he was in the wrong.

'You were the one who changed her mind when she was offered fifty thousand pounds,' he reminded her arrogantly, turning round to face her for the first time, the familiar coldness back in his eyes. 'Naturally, once I had assured myself that you and Saud had not been the victims of some kidnap plot, my first thought was . . .'

'That I had been the one doing the kidnapping,' Claire supplied bitterly for him, refusing to accept the validity of his explanations. Saud was his responsibility and a very heavy one as the natural inheritor of the Sheikh's titles and powers. 'Had I known you were likely to return, I would have left a message with Ali.'

Her gibe had gone home, she could see by the sudden tightening of his mouth, but if he chose to come and go at will, he could hardly expect to find her waiting patiently while he did so. 'As you can see for yourself, apart from having been fed with too many sweetmeats, Saud is quite well.' She held up the sleeping baby, his face still sticky and slightly grubby. 'Whatever you might think to the contrary, I do take my responsibilities towards Saud seriously,' Claire added on a quieter note, unable to bring herself to tell this hard, unyielding man how much she loved the little boy, so much that it was almost as though he were her own child.

'You have consistently shown a remarkable fondness for him,' Raoul agreed aloofly, spoiling it by adding cynically, 'but then when he is the heir to many thousands of millions of pounds, it is not hard to understand why.'

Anger made the colour bleed slowly from her face, leaving her as white as Raoul's robe. 'You think that,' she whispered painfully. 'You think me as vile and avaricious as that?'

'I think you are a woman whose devotion was bought for a mere fifty thousand pounds,' Raoul jeered at her hatefully. 'Oh, and by the way, I have a letter for you. From your lover no doubt. It was delivered to our Embassy in London and flown out with the rest of the mail. While you are living here as my wife, you will not receive letters from other men,' Raoul told her white-lipped, the sudden surge of anger she could see beating up behind his eyes frightening her with its intensity.

'What did you tell him when you wrote to him, Claire? That your bed was lonely and that you missed his caresses, so much so that you were quite prepared to take to your bed a man who is little better than a cross-bred mongrel, possessing the worst traits of both his parents? Oh yes, I know what is said about me,' he added tightly. 'Small children never spare the sensibilities or the pride of their peers.'

For one crazy moment she wanted to lean forward and smooth away what she was sure were lines of pain from beside his mouth, to hold him in her arms as she might have done Saud and comfort him, dispersing the hurt she could sense inside him, but the moment was destroyed as he flung her letter down on to the divan and walked through her room to the corridor that connected it with his own.

On this occasion there was no Ali to request that she join his master for dinner, and telling herself that she preferred it that way, Claire dismissed Zenaide when she had bathed and fed Saud, telling her maid that she was quite capable of preparing herself for bed. Zenaide still looked chastened and Claire hoped she had not been chastised for not telling Ali where they were going. Like an injured animal she wanted to retire to her lair to lick her wounds in peace.

How could Raoul have thought her so despicable? Surely he knew she would never do anything to hurt Saud? And as for his allegation that she might be deliberately fostering the child's affection for mercenary reasons ... Her mouth tightened and then relaxed as unbidden a memory slid into her mind of Teddy shortly after their parents had died. They had still been living in the old family house. She had spent the morning filling packing cases and Teddy was supposed to be playing outside in the garden. She had gone downstairs to make lunch and, on finding the front gate swinging open and no Teddy in sight, panic had exploded inside her. She had been on the point of calling the police when he had turned up three hours later, muddy and astonished that she should be so concerned. And yet instead of relief, all she had been able to feel had been a searing, blinding anger. She could well imagine Raoul's reaction to the news that they were both missing and perhaps his suspicions were understandable if one took the logical view.

Sighing faintly, Claire went through to the bathroom, filling the large marble tub with water scented with rose petals and relaxing into it while she read Teddy's letter.

Matron had taken him to buy some new clothes and he was to spend half-term with his friend 'Porky Rogers'. However, when she reached the final paragraph of his letter, Claire started to frown, a small gasp of dismay escaping her parted lips. Teddy wanted to know if he could spend part of the summer holidays in Omarah with her.

No! What on earth was she going to do? Having kept his existence such a secret from Raoul, she could hardly ask him now if her younger brother could come and stay with them. And Teddy was very astute for his age. She had allowed him to believe she had married for love. It wouldn't take Teddy long to discover what little regard Raoul had for his supposed wife. Hating to disappoint her brother but knowing there was little alternative, Claire tried to think of an adequate excuse. Perhaps she could tell him that she didn't have enough money for his flight. Yes, that would do it. She was always so chronically short of money that he would never suspect the truth. She would write to him later, and keep her fingers crossed that he wouldn't be too upset.

Back in her room, dressed in one of the soft silk

nightgowns Raoul had purchased for her in Paris, her hair a silver cloud on her shoulders, Claire found her thoughts returning to the scene in her room when they had returned from the oasis. Perhaps she ought to go and apologise to Raoul, and assure him that there was no question of her absconding with Saud. She could also tell him of her suspicions that his grandmother had suspected the truth. Not for one moment did she doubt the old lady, but it paid to be extra careful.

Before she could change her mind, or investigate her reasons too deeply, she shrugged on the soft peach negligee which matched her nightdress, unaware of how the silk-satin clung to her body, moulding itself lovingly to her curves, the soft peach fabric emphasising the silky pallor of her skin.

She knocked briefly on Raoul's door and hearing his voice pushed it open, puzzled when she saw that the room was empty, until she realised he was in the bathroom beyond. She heard him call out something in Arabic and as he emerged from the bathroom, a towel draped across his hips, his surprise at seeing her very evident as he frowned and pushed his fingers into the damp tangle of his hair.

'When I heard you knock I thought you were Ali. Is everything all right? Saud?' He sounded so formal and distant that Claire found herself wishing she had never been foolish enough to come to his room, on what she realised now was the flimsiest of pretexts and born more of her own need to be near him than any more logical motive.

'Saud's fine,' she assured him, dismayed by the husky, uneven pitch of her voice, dragging her eyes away from his gleaming torso, and the droplets of water still coursing hypnotically over his skin, darkening the tangle of hairs arrowing down over his flat belly. 'I just wanted to tell you that ... that I'd never do anything that might endanger him,' she managed, before panic overwhelmed her and she turned instinctively back towards the door, cursing the foolish impulse that had brought her into Raoul's presence.

'A pity you don't extend those sentiments to include yourself,' Raoul murmured softly, somehow reaching the door before her and leaning against it, blocking her exit, his mouth curling in a smile that increased her agitation. 'Because by coming to my room you have definitely endangered yourself, Claire, or is that what you had in mind? Did reading your lover's letter awaken a longing inside you that only a man's possession can assuage? This afternoon when I returned and found you gone, I wanted to seize your slender body in my arms and break it in two. But now my anger has found other channels and when it mingles with the desire I feel whenever you are close to me there is a dangerous alchemy between them. I want you, Claire,' he said softly, 'and by coming to my room you have admitted that you want me too.'

'No.' Her denial was a strangled protest which he ignored, smothering the sound with the raging heat of his mouth which told her that he hadn't exaggerated the dangerous chain reaction she had set off inside him. His tongue forced her lips to part, hotly exploring the hidden recesses of her mouth, compelling her to give him the fervid response his kiss demanded, and by doing so feed his desire.

'Too many times I have wanted you like this,' he muttered thickly, sliding his fingers into her hair and curling the silver strands round them. 'My desire for you is like a leech sucking at my life blood and my reason, and until I assuage it I cannot be free. You arouse me to a lust I heartily despise,' he continued, each word a poisoned barb in her heart, 'but I know if you tried to leave this room now I would come after you and drag you back to my bed, and even perhaps enjoy doing so. Strange that such a pale, golden beauty should arouse the darker side of desire.'

The darker side of desire. Claire shuddered deeply, trying to wrench her mouth away from the renewed possession of his, telling herself that she would despise herself to the end of her days if she gave in to the tug of sensation she could feel exploding through her now. He had told her quite plainly what he wanted, how he felt about her, but if she aroused dark, dangerous passions in him, he aroused a blind need in her that would not listen to reason or logic, and her fingers, encountering the hard smoothness of his body, could no more be stopped in their wanton exploration of his skin than her heart could be prevented from beating.

He quickly disposed of her negligee, stroking the liquid softness of her body until she was shivering delicately in his arms, welcoming the fierce, almost brutal urgency of his kisses, even though his hunger bruised her mouth and through her delirium a small voice warned that there could be only one outcome. It was with relief that she felt him remove her nightgown and carry her to his bed, her body stretched languorously on the silk covers as he stood over her, shrugging aside his towel. His body was totally male, his stomach flat and his lean hips narrow; her fingertips automatically followed the path of her eyes down his body, the hard tautness of his buttocks and the muscled solidity of his thighs, darkly shadowed with soft hair. He turned and she caught her breath, half-awed and half-dismayed by the aroused maleness of his body as he moved towards her, his fingertips drifting upwards over her body with far more assurance and knowledge in their touch than she felt she could ever possess.

'You want me. Tell me it's true,' he urged, as he came down alongside her, taking her in his arms, his mouth finding the vulnerable area behind her ear and teasing it until she was trembling against him, gasping out that she wanted him more than she wanted life itself.

'As bad as that?' He almost seemed to purr with satisfaction and alarm shot through the haze of sexual need engulfing her. This was wrong. She might love him but he most certainly did not love her, and worse still she suspected he was going to be very angry when he discovered that she was still a virgin. It occurred to her that she ought to tell him, but his hands were doing such delicious things to her body, his mouth and tongue were inciting such a fevered response from her that she felt incapable of discussing anything at all, much less something that would surely put a stop to his expert love making.

'Still want me?' His tongue teased her erect nipples and she raked her nails protestingly across his back, the tempo of his lovemaking suddenly changing as his body tensed against her, his mouth now avid in the demands it made on her body as his hands slid to her hips and his knee parted her thighs.

The intrusion of his body was unexpectedly painful, making her tense, her eyes widening in shock, the deep kiss she had been enjoying broken as she pulled instinctively away. But Raoul was still holding her hips and his possession continued even though she cried out to him to stop, her world turning from pleasure to a pain she fought instinctively against.

Something was different, but what? Slowly, Claire opened her eyes and then closed them again as reality hit her like a bath of icy water. She was still in Raoul's bed. She moved gingerly, feeling his body close to her and winced as she remembered his anger. Mercifully, she had passed out before he had been able to give full vent to it. He was asleep now, if she turned her head carefully she could see him. The lamp which was still illuminated threw dark shadows across his face. Even in sleep he looked hard and unyielding and she shuddered sickly, remembering what had happened.

Dear God, how could she have been so ... so stupid? No wonder he had been angry. She bit her lips, her face flaming as she remembered some of the comments he had flung at her. She had wanted to leave then, she rememberd, but as she had sat up the room swayed muzzily round her and he had pushed her back unceremoniously telling her to lie still. And that had not been the worst. Even though her mind shied away from it, she forced herself to remember how he had left the bed and come back with a sponge and some towels and had made her lie there while he soothed away the worst of the pain. She didn't think she could forget until her dying day how grim and furious he had looked. Never, as long as she lived, would she ever endure anything quite as humiliating. That at least was something to be thankful for, she told herself drily. She had acted like the heroine out of a Victorian romance, swooning away because a man had . . .

'How are you feeling?'

Raoul was awake! Colour burned up under her skin. Why, oh why had he insisted that she remain here with him? Still, she would have had to have faced him some time. Perhaps it was as well to get it over and done with now.

'I . . . I'm fine, thank you,' she said quickly, edging towards the edge of the bed. 'In fact, I think I'd better go back to my own room, Saud might wake.'

'No.' His hand shot out, his fingers imprisoning her wrist. 'Not yet. I've been lying here waiting for you to wake up.'

He had? Misgivings smote her. Why? So that he could lecture her again? Hadn't it all already been said?

'I'm sorry.' Heavens, why was she apologising? He ought to be the one doing that. But then, of course, men did not expect to find themselves with an inexperienced virgin in their bed these days.

'So am I,' Raoul agreed evenly, 'but what's done is done. You must have been missing your boy-friend very badly, although he'll hardly be gratified to learn what form your frustration took.'

Claire had to bite down hard on her lip to stop herself from crying. 'I . . . I must go back to my own room,' she protested again. She suddenly felt weak and shaky, and wanted to put as great a distance as possible between Raoul's powerful body and her own frailer one. As though he read her mind he turned towards her, cupping her face with his free hand.

'I'm sorry if it didn't live up to all your maidenly expectations. It was quite a shock for me too, you know.' He saw her expression and laughed derisively. 'Oh yes, it isn't exactly a turn-on to find the woman in your arms is crying with pain and not pleasure. Not unless you're a sadist, that is, which I am not. Do you still want me?'

Claire could only stare at him, her disbelief showing openly in her eyes. He laughed again, his thumb rubbing slowly along her jaw. 'But you did want me,' he reminded her softly, 'you told me so, and I wanted you.'

'But that was . . .'

'Before I hurt you?' He bent towards her and Claire could see the smoky flames burning in his eyes. 'What happened was unfortunate, but it needn't be a tragedy. I suppose I should have guessed, but your response to me was so complete that I took you for an experienced sensualist.' He bent his head, capturing the frantic pulse beating at the base of her throat, and stroking his fingers along her flesh as though he enjoyed the vulnerability of her skin beneath them. 'No . . . keep still,' he told her when she tried to struggle. 'I'm not going to hurt you.'

She moved, and anger suddenly blazed in his eyes. 'Damn you,' he swore suddenly, 'have you any idea what it was like to see the fear and pain in your eyes? Why didn't you tell me, you stubborn little fool? But I will see pleasure in your eyes, Claire,' he added softly, 'and before dawn pearls the desert sky. You will melt beneath my touch and murmur your pleasure against my skin.'

He pushed back the covers he had heaped over her, exposing the full length of her body to his probing gaze, his hands moving slowly over her skin. She wouldn't respond, she couldn't respond, Claire thought numbly. What was the point when it would only end in pain? But against her will his touch communicated a wanton need to her nerve-endings, his slow caresses stimulating a desire she was surprised she could still feel.

'Touch me, Claire,' Raoul murmured against her ear, nibbling the lobe with sharp teeth. 'Wouldn't you like to touch me as I am touching you?'

Of course she wouldn't, but somehow she was, the tension expelled from her body on a soft sigh as his coaxing fingers drifted against her breast, stroking the rounded flesh gently so that Claire found it impossible to tell where acceptance ended and need began. So gradually that she was barely aware of what was happening, her body began to respond until it was no longer enough simply to lie in Raoul's arms letting him caress her, she wanted to touch him too. His skin burned strangely beneath her lips, moist with a perspiration she hadn't expected. The small satisfied sounds of pleasure he made as she touched him gave her the courage to go on, touching him more intimately, letting her tongue brush teasingly over his flat male nipples, half-exultant and half-shocked by his immediate response.

'I think I was right first time,' Raoul mutterd hoarsely, pulling away from her. 'You are a sensualist.' His fingers touched her thigh, moving along the tender inner flesh, his eyes locked on hers as he witnessed her involuntary response before she remembered her earlier pain and tensed in panic, trying to push him away, her heart thudding erratically until he moved, soothing her with light kisses until her fear was lost beneath a rising tide of need. Something was happening to her, something she hadn't believed possible when she opened her eyes less than half an hour ago; and when Raoul's hand returned to her thigh she only tensed momentarily, her fear forgotten as his tongue teased her nipples until her fingers tightened in his hair and she was abandonedly urging his mouth against her, her hands leaving his hair to clasp the smooth muscles of his back as he tugged gently on the aching peaks of her breasts.

Suddenly it wasn't enough simply to feel the contraction and expansion of his muscles under her fingers, she wanted to touch and taste every part of his body. A wild, heated urgency flooded out fear, even when Raoul's fingers stroked upwards, touching her intimately, making her gasp and tense and then relax beneath their knowledgeable caress. Her small teeth bit urgently into his skin, feeling his shoulder muscles clench and his body harden, pleasure banishing fear as she strove to communicate to him the delight he was giving her.

'Touch me. Kiss me, Claire,' he muttered thickly, punctuating his words with hard kisses, taking her hand and placing it against his body, kissing her fiercely as a shudder of pleasure rippled through him.

Fear left her completely, the soft kisses she pressed against Raoul's body eliciting a response that surprised and awed her.

'You don't even begin to know what you're doing to me, do you?' he demanded rawly, holding her slightly away from him. 'This began as an exercise in showing you that making love doesn't go hand in hand with pain, but when you touch me my body forgets you're only one step away from being a virgin and knows only that the softness of your hands and lips against it is a sweet form of torture.'

He kissed her again, more deeply this time until she felt as though she were sinking into soft warm darkness, the coaxing stroke of his fingers against the most vulnerable, intimate part of her body making her tremble and ache, her hands making feverish forays against his skin until he groaned and pressed himself against her, his flesh hot and damp, his skin tasting salt beneath her tongue. But it was only when his caresses had elicited a rhythmic unfamiliar reaction from her body that he gave in to the urgent need she could feel in the hard thrust of his body against her, this time drawing her slowly against him, teasing her breasts with light tormenting kisses as his body moved fluidly against hers, slowly possessing it, urging her to touch and experience the pulsating life force of him, until her touch became surer and communicated to him the same rhythmic welcome as her body, his mouth closing hotly over first the hard peak of one breast and then the other as she moaned and moved urgently beneath him, encouraged by the soft words of praise he murmured in her ear and then by the hard demand of his mouth as he relinquished his control, abandoning it to the driving force of his body.

His fierce cry of pleasure was an unfamiliar and yet elemental sound exploding around them as she dissolved into a whirlpool of pleasure, unaware that she was calling his name until he kissed and soothed her, unaware of anything other than the experience they had just shared.

CHAPTER SEVEN

WHEN Claire woke up she was aware of having slept well and deeply. She was alone but still in Raoul's bed, and she leapt out, hurrying into her own room, her cheeks darkly flushed as she saw Zenaide waiting patiently for her, playing with Saud.

'The Lord Raoul said to let you sleep,' she said easily, 'he also gave instructions that I was to prepare you for a journey. See . . .' she indicated a case on the bed. 'I have packed what he instructed.'

Claire's eyes widened in appalled comprehension. Raoul was sending her away! She had betrayed her love to him and now he was sending her away from him. But what about Saud? Perhaps if she pleaded with him he would allow her to stay. What had happened was not entirely her fault. Her skin flushed delicately as she remembered her abandoned response to him. But he was the one who had encouraged that response. He had wanted her as much as she had wanted him, but now he was obviously regretting that wanting and wished only to be rid of her.

Saud beamed up at her, holding up his arms, and she bent down automatically to pick him up, tears suddenly blinding her as she realised that this was possibly the last time she would hold the little boy. What would the Sheikh say when he learned what Raoul had done? How would Raoul himself explain away her absence? But then it was easy for Muslim men to divorce women they no longer wanted, wasn't it? Tired, muddled thoughts chased one another through her mind. Too proud to go to Raoul and beg him to allow her to stay, even for Saud's sake, she numbly allowed Zenaide to bully her gently into getting bathed and dressed, glad that she had sent the younger girl to look after Saud when she saw the beginnings of dark bruises staining her skin—the unmistakable signs of the passion which had over- whelmed Raoul at the height of their love making.

Shivering suddenly as she wrapped her body in the thick fleecy towel Zenaide had provided, Claire wondered a little about that love making. The first time she could understand. Raoul had been bitterly, furiously angry and she was not so naïve that she couldn't appreciate how quickly desire could spring from the loins of anger, once at least. But afterwards, when his anger had had time to die down ... He had still wanted her, Claire reminded herself bleakly, and he had decided to assuage that want, desire at that particular moment in time being more important to him than anything else. But later, with his hunger appeased, he would have thought differently. Besides, if she was honest with herself, he had never wanted her to partner him in this charade and she, fool that she was, had given him the perfect excuse to be rid of her. What would he tell his uncle? That she had fallen in love with him, and he found her love embarrassing?

'If the Sitt is ready, Ali is waiting to drive her to the airport.'

Heeding Zenaide's calm warning, Claire dressed quickly, donning the clothes Zenaide had put out for her—soft, pure silk underwear in warm cream and a silk dress in the same fabric with a matching unstructured jacket. The ensemble was a sophisticated one, a little too dressy to travel in, but she felt too weary and miserable to change it. When she walked back into her bedroom she saw on the bed the perky hat that went with the outfit. In the shop she had loved it, but now . . . However, Zenaide was placing it with the rest of her luggage. If nothing else, she was better off by an exclusive brand-new wardrobe, she reminded herself cynically, trying to ignore the inner voice adding that she was also coming close to having a broken heart. She loved Raoul. She couldn't deny it any longer. With one last kiss for Saud, her lips were trembling badly as she turned to embrace Zenaide. 'You will look after him, Zenaide, won't you?'

'The Lord Raoul has arranged everything,' Zenaide assured her. 'He will not be left alone for so much as a moment.'

In that, at least, she had faith in Raoul. He would never let anything injure Saud. But what of love? Would the little boy have that?

A servant placed her case in the car. Raoul was so eager to get rid of her that there hadn't been time to pack everything, but doubtless the rest of her wardrobe would be sent on after her. Just before she left she had slipped in to Raoul's room, trying not to look at the large bed as she placed the jewellery he had given her beside it.

All the way to the airport she was fighting for self-control, trying to force back the tears that, once started, wouldn't cease until she had cried herself dry. As before, there were no passport formalities to endure. Ali escorted her through the departure hall and out on to the tarmac where a streamlined jet plane waited, bearing the colours of the Omarah royal family. Her mouth twisted in a bitter smile, Claire mounted the stairs. Raoul was so anxious to get rid of her that he wouldn't even wait for the twice-weekly Concorde flight, and she shuddered to think how much it would cost to transport her back to London in this expensive rich man's toy.

A steward showed her to a seat. Unlike a commercial plane, this one was furnished more like a luxurious living-room with deep lush seats and a separate section which he told her contained a bedroom and bathroom.

They were airborne almost immediately, the blue waters of the gulf left behind below them as the plane levelled out. The steward had disappeared and yet now, when she had the privacy to cry, Claire found that her pain went deeper than mere tears. She wanted to cry but it just wasn't possible. Instead her body ached with feverish pain, her mind crawling round in circles as she tried to rationalise the agony of mind and emotions threatening to swamp her. She heard a door open, and anticipated the return of the steward, but instead it was Raoul who stood over her, bending down to speak to her, his face stern and somehow older as he said something that seemed to reach her through a dizzy haze. He turned away then and she closed her eyes thinking he must be a mirage conjured up by her yearning mind, but there was nothing illusionary about the brandy he forced her to swallow, or the anger she could see glittering bleakly in his eyes as he returned the glass to the hovering steward.

'Claire, are you all right now?'

'Perfectly,' she lied in a thin, little voice. 'It was just that seeing you gave me such a shock. But then I suppose I ought to have guessed. I suppose you're here to make sure that I actually leave ... I'm tired, Raoul,' she lied again, turning her face towards the window. 'I think I'll try and get some sleep. Wake me up when we reach Heathrow,' she finished sardonically.

'We aren't going to Heathrow.'

The quiet words were like a douche of cold water. 'Not ... Then ...'

'We're flying to Paris, Claire,' Raoul told her in the same cold emotionless voice, glancing at his watch, the gold strap glinting in the light, as he added, 'where we shall be married at five o'clock this evening. Everything is arranged. I have your passport, and I have checked with your Embassy. Since I possess dual citizenship and have retained my Christian religion, there is no bar to our civil marriage being performed in Paris. I have arranged matters with as much discretion as possible. Officially, we are travelling to Paris because my father has been taken ill, and you, in your capacity as my wife, have persuaded me to be reconciled with him.' His mouth tightened a little. 'My father has, of course, had to be included in my plans. He expressed himself most willing to participate in my charade ...'

'Married? You and I? But ...'

'Surely you did not think there could be any other outcome after what passed between us? Even now you might be carrying my child. Do you honestly think I would allow him to be brought up as I was, not knowing the love and care of his father?'

'Your child? But . . .'

'But what?' he asked sardonically. 'But it is not possible? On the contrary, Claire, it is all too possible! And our marriage need not be without its compensations. Sexually, at least, we are compatible, even if you do love another . . .'

Claire's head was reeling. Did he honestly still think she loved someone else, after what had happened between them? Even if he did, she suspected it would not be long before he guessed the truth, and dredging up every last ounce of her courage, she said firmly, 'No, Raoul, I will not marry you.'

'And I say you will.' His eyes had darkened to jade and Claire felt a *frisson* of fear as she looked into their obsidian depths. 'And I mean what I say. You will marry me, even if I have to drug and bind you to get you to the altar. Is that the way you want it, Claire?'

He wasn't lying. He had every intention of carrying out his threat if she didn't agree, and all because of a slender chance that she might be carrying his child.

'It seems a rather drastic course of action to take simply because we've been lovers,' she pointed out drily. 'We don't even like one another . . .'

'And I am the one to blame for this state of affairs because I gave in to my physical need of you, is that what you are trying to say?' His face darkened, the skin melding itself to his hard bones. 'You, Claire, are you not equally responsible? Do you think for one moment that if you had told me that you were still a virgin I . . .'

'But you did,' Claire reminded him hotly, his angry words unleashing her own temper. 'Afterwards you . . .'

'I am a man, not a boy, Claire,' he cut in jeeringly. 'What did you expect me to do? Carry you back to your own bed when every part of me still clamoured for release? But what is done is done and we must now think of the future. Our future and that of the child you might be carrying.'

There was no way she could make him listen to reason, Claire thought despairingly, and bearing in mind the traumas of his own childhood, was it so hard to understand why he was so determined that they should marry? He was, after all, right; impossible though it felt at the moment, she could be carrying his child. Taking a deep breath, Claire made up her mind what course of action she must take.

'Very well, Raoul, I will marry you,' she agreed with a calm she was far from feeling, 'but only if you give me your word that until we know whether I am pregnant or not, we live ... separately, and that if I am not carrying your child you will divorce me.'

'And if you are carrying my child?'

'Then . . .'

'Then you will still want a divorce, even knowing you must leave your child with me, is that it? How you must love him, this man who holds your heart, even though it is I who have possessed your body. Very well,' he said tautly, 'it shall be as you wish, with one further stipulation. There will be no divorce until Saud is out of danger. Do you agree?'

Saud! She had almost forgotten him in the trauma of more recent events. 'And if I do will you . . .?'

'Allow you to sleep alone in your own bed?' His eyebrows rose. 'You are letting your imagination run away with you, Claire. What happened between us last night happened, but you have my word that while you live under my roof, whatever hungers and appetites I might have, I will not seek to satiate them in your bed. Does that reassure you?'

Numbly she nodded her head, turning away so that he wouldn't see the pain in her eyes. Of course, she should have expected nothing more. Raoul was a man of the East, accustomed to satisfying his physical desires with women who would be pliant and accepting in his arms. She had been nothing more than a brief aberration which already he was regretting.

Please God, don't let there be a child, she prayed mentally. If she was to bear Raoul's child, how on earth could she bring herself to leave them; and how could she stay, falling deeper in love with Raoul every day and knowing that her love could never be returned? Perhaps even one day being forced to witness his love for someone else? Had he loved the Muslim girl he had nearly been betrothed to?

They were married quietly and discreetly later that afternoon in a suburb of Paris. Not the wedding she had always envisaged for herself. As they had stepped off the plane, Raoul had turned back and then reappeared, handing her the large box in which Zenaide had placed her hat as they stepped into the waiting car.

'It is perhaps not the bridal array you might have expected, but I asked Zenaide to pack it for you.'

As he had asked her maid to put out the cream suit, Claire wondered, stealing a brief look at his shuttered profile, before taking the hat from its box. It was true, it did make her look more bridal, but her heart was heavy when the car came to a stop outside the small town-hall where the wedding ceremony was to be performed.

Now it was over and they were man and wife, Raoul's gold ring glittering on her finger. Outside their car still waited, the engine purring almost soundlessly. The brief ceremony had taken little more than fifteen minutes, and as Raoul replaced their passports and marriage certificate inside his jacket, Claire stared numbly ahead. Fifteen minutes. That was all it had taken to change the course of her life. Automatically her hand crept to the reassuring flatness of her stomach.

'Praying your body is not cherishing my seed?' Raoul demanded harshly. 'Try to look on the bright side, Claire. If you are carrying my child you may be sure that you will be generously recompensed for the ... inconvenience.' His lip curled disdainfully, and Claire was overwhelmed by the need to lash out and hurt him as he had wounded her.

'That's your answer to everything, isn't it?' she stormed at him. 'Money ... Well, there are some things money can't wipe out. I don't want your money, Raoul. I don't want anything of yours!'

'Especially not my child.'

The words lay between them like a gage, but Claire was too bitter to back down now. 'Especially not that,' she agreed, watching the anger die out of his eyes to be replaced by a cold, blank dislike.

He leaned forward and said something to their driver, then settled himself back in his seat without another word. Claire longed to ask him where they were going and how long he intended them to remain in Paris. Already she was missing Saud. Her hand covered her stomach again. What would it be like to have Raoul's child? In other circumstances, if there was the merest chance that he might return her love, there was nothing that would bring her greater happiness, but as it was she dreaded the prospect of finding herself pregnant. For the rest of her life she would be torn in two. Torn between wanting and loving her child, and knowing that if she stayed with it she would be risking the untold anguish of living in proximity to Raoul, thirsting more and more with every day that passed for his love, like a man separated from an oasis by a thick glass wall. How could she possibly endure it?

Their car slid to a halt, jerking her out of her thoughts. They were outside a hospital, and Raoul got out, politely opening Claire's door, his hand on her elbow as he escorted her inside.

'We are in Paris to visit my father, remember?' he murmured as they walked into a tiled reception area decorated lavishly with flowers. The receptionist greeted them with a smile, her eyes widening fractionally as she looked at Raoul. No matter where he went, he would always draw those looks of appreciation from her sex, Claire recognised, the ache in her heart increasing. They were directed down a corridor and Raoul paused outside the room they had been told was his father's.

Lucien D'Albro was sitting up in bed reading a book, and he greeted them both with a smile. 'I had not realised that being in hospital could be such a pleasant experience,' he said to Claire, his eyes twinkling. 'One has every comfort. Indeed one might almost be in the most luxurious of hotels, and then of course, there is the added bonus of the nurses. So,' he turned to Raoul, 'it is done?'

'Yes.' Raoul kept his back to his father and walked across to the window. 'I have not yet thanked you for the part you have played in this. Time was short and there was no one else I could ask . . .'

His voice was low, the words terse and bitten off, but Claire was facing Lucien and was able to see the pain in his eyes as he said quietly, 'Is it so very hard to come to me when you need help, Raoul? I am after all your father . . .'

'Genetically, yes,' Raoul agreed harshly, 'but as a child . . .'

'It was your mother's wish that she return to her people. She wanted me to go with her, but my work, my life, was here in Paris. I explained that to her when we married. My tour in Omarah was only a brief one. She knew that once it was over I would be returning to France. I did not want to let you go, Raoul, but she reminded me how much more her people could give you than I. Our name is an ancient one, but financially . . .' He spread his hands. 'It was no secret that I married your mother for financial security. I had intended to use her dowry to restore the family château. It had been the dream of my father,' he sighed.

'You are lying,' Raoul interrupted angrily. My mother told me how you used her dowry—in gambling, escorting other women, living the life of a wealthy playboy.'

'No. You are wrong. That is how I made my *living*.'

There was a tense silence, and Claire wondered if she ought to leave them alone. She had a feeling that what was about to be said in the privacy of this room was something between father and son alone, but even as she made a move to leave Lucien grasped her wrist.

'No, Claire, please stay,' he said gently. 'If what Raoul tells me is true it could well be that you carry my grandchild.' He smiled when she blushed. 'I must confess I suspected all along that you were not the mother of Saud. You looked too innocent . . . and far too unknowing to have been the lover of a man like my son. I hope you will learn well from my mistakes, Raoul. I should never have let your mother take you, but I was tired of having her wealth thrown in my face. When she left I made a vow that I wouldn't touch a penny of her dowry and I haven't. Shortly after she had gone, I became ill and I lost my position in the Ministry. When I recovered I had to make a living somehow. I had always been lucky as a gambler.'

He shrugged his broad shoulders. 'You know the rest. The château still stands, but only just. I have willed it to you, together with your mother's money. Both are, after all, yours by right. Perhaps in time you will bring my son to Paris again, Claire, this time with the true purpose of effecting a reconciliation between us. Never let pride stand in the way of your happiness, my son,' he said quietly to Raoul.

They left the hospital in silence, Claire not daring to look at Raoul. How had he taken his father's revelations? That Lucien had spoken the truth Claire did not doubt, but it would take more than verbal explanations to cure the wounds of the past that still went very deep with Raoul.

They stayed once more at the George V, occupying the same suite they had had before. When Claire asked uncertainly if it was possible to telephone the palace to check up on Saud, Raoul glanced at her curiously. 'One might almost suppose you were genuinely fond of that child . . .'

'Why shouldn't I be?' Claire responded bitterly. 'Oh, I know you think my affection for him springs from avarice, but you are wrong. I was instrumental in saving his life,' she said almost to herself. 'I feel almost as though he is my child . . .'

'And yet feeling like that you are prepared to desert your own child, because he is also mine?' he threw at her harshly. 'How you must hate me, Claire. Why? Because I took from you that which you were saving for another? Or is there more to it than that? Is it not simply that I took, but that I gave too, more pleasure than you can ever hope to find in the arms of your cold English lover, who does not even want you enough to storm the citadel of your virginity . . .'

He had gone before she could think of a fitting enough retort to silence him, and it was well after midnight when Claire heard the door to their suite opening quietly. Where had he been all evening? With someone else? The thought was like a knife thrust in her heart.

Two days later they were back in Omarah, but this time she was in reality Raoul's wife. 'Saud has missed you,' Zenaide told her. 'He will be glad that you are back.' There was a small piece in one of the French papers about Raoul's visit to the bedside of his supposedly sick father, which Raoul pointed out to her one evening after he had returned from the city.

His business responsibilities kept him very fully occupied. Claire learned from Zenaide that it was Raoul and the Sheikh who had been responsible for the intensive reorganisation of the education system, so that girls as well as boys could benefit from the wealth that oil had brought to the small state.

A conference in London necessitated his leaving for that capital at the end of their first week of marriage, and as she watched him leave, Claire couldn't help wondering how he would spend his nights when he was away. She had no illusions. Any number of beautiful women would be only to glad to sleep with Raoul, even without the added allure of his wealth.

As yet there was no evidence that she might be carrying his child, and Claire was glad that she had stipulated that they were not to live as man and wife. Raoul was cynical enough to be perfectly able to make love to her without caring about her, but her frail spirit was already too overburdened to be able to take the strain of a relationship with too much love on one side and none on the other.

After a morning spent on the beach, Claire returned with Saud to the palace for lunch and then a sleep. She had found herself falling into the pattern of sleeping in the afternoon when the sun was at its hottest, and today she felt particularly tired. It was a steep walk down to the beach, and as she walked back up she visualised Raoul's Moorish ancestors carrying their human prizes back up to the palace—young European girls destined for the slave markets of the East, vast amounts of gold and precious jewels from

Spanish galleons, fair-haired, fair-skinned girls stolen from the English coast. How would she have felt had she been in their shoes?

She shuddered, putting Saud down as a wave of dizziness made her cling to the solid support of the cliff face. She must have walked up the path too quickly, she chided herself when the world had righted itself and Saud's plaintive cries reminded her of his presence. He beamed when she picked him up, proudly displaying his two new teeth. Poor Saud, who had lost both mother and father, and who for all the wealth he would one day inherit was a pauper indeed when it came to the riches of love.

There had been no more visitors to the palace, and Zenaide had explained that it was normal to leave newly-weds alone for one full month after the marriage ceremony.

'Blessed is the bride who can tell her family at the end of that time that she carries her husband's child.' She blushed rosily, glancing at Saud who lay kicking on the bed, revelling in the freedom from his nappy, and Claire guessed what she was thinking. Zenaide, at least, did not doubt that Saud was her child.

Once again Claire ate alone. She had found her appetite diminishing since their return from Paris. The heat seemed to sap her energy despite the efficiency of the air-conditioning installed in the palace. She was often lethargic and dull. She needed some activity to occupy her mind, she acknowledged. If she had really been Raoul's chosen wife she could have approached him with the problem. There must be many areas in which she could help. He had mentioned entertaining various representatives from other countries and Claire knew from Zenaide that he had an apartment in the city in one wing of the Sheikh's palace. She was not used to inactivity.

She picked up the letter she had received from her godmother, wincing as she read of her pleasure in her marriage. If only she knew the truth! Sighing, Claire folded the thick paper, suddenly remembering Teddy's unanswered letter. Where on earth was it? She must write to him telling him that it would be impossible for him to come out and stay with them. She would do it first thing in the morning, she thought to herself as she prepared for bed.

The night was hot, even the thin silk of her gown uncomfortable against her skin, sleep somehow eluding her as she tossed and turned in the wide bed. Where was Raoul now? Who was he with?

She tensed as she heard Saud cry. He didn't normally wake up during the night, and Claire listened to his cries for several minutes, warning herself that it would be foolish to go into him, but when they persisted she flung back the covers of her bed, pulling on a silk robe and hurrying through into Saud's room.

The panda which was his favourite toy was on the floor and Claire bent to pick it up guessing that it had been the cause of the commotion. Saud had seen her and crawled eagerly to the bars of his cot, grinning at her in the darkness. It was as she kneeled in front of him, the panda in one hand, the other steadying herself, that Claire first heard the noise. No more than a soft slither, it sent such a shudder of dread through her that she couldn't move. Saud chuckled, obviously thinking he was participating in some new game, his chuckles turning to wails of protest when she didn't move.

The room was so dark. If only she had switched on the lamp when she came in, Claire thought feverishly, trying to shush Saud, her ears stretched for that slithering sound which she prayed and hoped had been nothing more than a figment of an overworked imagination. But no ... There it was again. Louder this time, closer, relentless. Perspiration broke out all over her body. Dear God, there was a snake somewhere in the room with them. Numbly, she tried to remember what Zenaide had told her about local snakes. There were several varieties, one particularly deadly, but how could she remember which was which? She couldn't even see it and even if she could, she was so panic-stricken that she doubted she could have told the difference between a rattlesnake and a common grass-snake.

Saud was trying to drag himself to his feet using the cot rails, and Claire froze as she heard the sibilant slither again. The thing was in Saud's cot, tangled up somewhere among his covers. A scream clawed at her throat but she suppressed it, her whole body trembling as she straightened slowly, not knowing where the danger lay, expecting with every second to feel sharp fangs biting into her skin—hers or Saud's! He was sleeping dressed only in a nappy because it had been so hot, and Claire felt as chilled as though she had been standing in an Arctic wind as she visualised the thing in the cot with him. Even now as he struggled to stand, beaming at her in the semi-darkness, it could be positioning itself to strike.

The pictures conjured up by her mind were too much for her. Not giving herself time to think, Claire darted towards the cot lifting him out. He whimpered in fright as though sensing her terror and as she clasped him against her, Claire heard another blood-freezing sound from his cot. It was too much. Trembling all over, she opened her mouth and started to scream, weak tears of terror pouring down her cheeks. The bedroom door was flung back on its hinges, the light blinding her as it snapped on.

'Claire . . .'

Raoul's voice roused her from her panic, her eyes opening and noting the dark trousers he was wearing, and the shirt unbuttoned almost to the waist as though she had interrupted him on the point of undressing. She hadn't realised he was back, but as he took a step towards her, his forehead pleated in a deep frown, she remembered what had happened and called out, 'No, Raoul . . . don't come too close. I think there's a . . . a snake in Saud's cot.'

She shuddered as she spoke, closing her eyes as she averted her face from the pretty blue and white cot they had bought in Paris. Never would she be able to look at it in the same way again. 'I heard him crying,' she added huskily, as Raoul continued to stare from her to the cot as though unable to believe what she was saying. 'I came in, and . . . and I could hear something moving. It seemed to come from the cot.' She was white and shaking with reaction, her frenzied, 'No, Raoul, please don't . . .' halting him on his way towards her. 'You might get bitten,' she added hoarsely as he looked at her.

'You come here to me then,' he said compellingly, using the same soothing tone he might have used to a terrified child. He didn't believe her, Claire thought sickly, as she took first one and then another step past the cot.

A sudden movement froze her, an angry hiss, and the dark, reed-like body emerged from the sheets, poised, watching, mesmerising her with its dark, glittering eyes. Dimly she heard Raoul curse, and then move, almost knocking her off her feet as he pushed her away, plucking the thing from the soft blue cotton. It squirmed through the air, landing on the floor, and Raoul's shoe crushed down on the back of its neck. Sickened but unable to tear her eyes away, Claire watched its dying writhing, its poison sacs emptying on to the floor, all movement slowly going.

'It's over,' she heard Raoul saying quietly. 'It's over Claire. You're both quite safe now. Come . . .'

Numbly she walked towards him, letting him take her hand and lead her back into her own room, feeling all the time as though she were sitting on the sidelines outside her body, watching its slow movements.

Her false calm broke when Saud started to cry, fierce tremors seizing her body. She was aware of Raoul taking Saud from her, the little boy finding comfort in the hard pressure of his arms; and then it was her turn, her face was pressed against the hard warmth of his bare chest as he put Saud down and comforted her.

'It's all over now, Claire. You're both quite safe,' he repeated, but Claire didn't feel safe. She felt distinctly vulnerable, her body aching with pain and need, her body treacherously conscious of Raoul's proximity, of the satiny feel of his skin beneath her trembling fingers, the dark hairs crisp against her palm, his heartbeat a reassuring thud against her.

'How could it have got in there?' she begged, her teeth chattering with reaction. 'Raoul, someone must know about Saud. Someone tried to kill him . . .' Her voice started to rise and she felt Raoul's fingers at her nape, urging her to relax against him.

'Perhaps,' he agreed, 'but maybe not. Whichever the case, it was fortunate that you went in to him.'

'He had thrown his panda on the floor,' Claire told him stupidly, knowing that she was simply talking to hold at bay the terrible fear still stalking her. 'I was just going to give it to him when I heard it. Oh Raoul, he could have died. I could have gone in there in the morning and . . .'

Her stomach heaved and she shuddered in his calming embrace. 'Shush . . . you mustn't torture yourself with too-vivid imaginings. It is true that it could have happened, but it is also true that it didn't. Allah must be over Saud.'

He said it half-humorously, but Claire wasn't in the mood to be amused. She glanced fearfully at her own bed, and correctly interpreting her fear, Raoul released her, carefully stripping it and then remaking it. Not until he had searched every inch of the room and assured her that it was safe did he return to her.

'If you would like me to stay with you for tonight . . . I should prefer what has happened to be kept a secret between us. If it was a deliberate attempt to kill Saud, then whoever made it will try again. I don't want to panic them into going into hiding. If we say nothing it might lull them into a false sense of security. Curiosity to discover how their plan misfired, if nothing else, should draw them out into the open.'

Did she want him to stay with her? If only he knew

how much, Claire thought wildly. There was nothing she wanted more right now than the security of his arms round her, his body shielding hers. A slow heat started to burn through her, amazing her that she could so easily feel desire alongside her fear. It wasn't merely for security and protection that she wanted Raoul beside her, she thought bleakly. She wanted the passionate possession of his body as well, his hands and lips against her skin, hers against his. She became acutely conscious of the warmth of his skin, of the thinness of her silk gown and her breasts hardening perceptibly beneath it, aroused by their contact with his body. Trying to disengage herself, Claire said wildly, 'I didn't think you were coming back tonight, I . . .'

'My business was completed earlier than I expected,' Raoul told her tersely, adding with a cruelty that hurt, 'besides, where else would I want to be other than with my wife; the woman who might bear my child?'

His hand covered her stomach, heating her skin until she felt fluid and boneless, his lips brushed hers lightly until they parted voluntarily.

'Go to sleep, Claire,' Raoul told her harshly, releasing her with an obvious rejection that stung. 'Otherwise I might forget my side of our bargain and take you to my bed.' He saw her expression and laughed sardonically. 'What's the matter? Do you find it offensive when I remind you of my frustration . . . my physical needs? Do I shock you with my blunt admission that I want you? Go to bed, Claire,' he reiterated, turning towards the door, and it struck her that he looked tired, and more than that, defeated. But there was no reason for him to suffer the demons of sexual frustration, she told herself bitterly. There must be women aplenty who would delight in his lovemaking.

Too exhausted to dwell more deeply on his comments Claire crawled into her bed, but she didn't sleep well. Almost every half-hour she was awake and checking on Saud, who Raoul had insisted she return to his cot, which he assured her was now quite safe. The snake had also been removed, but she couldn't pass the spot where it had lain without shuddering with fear and nausea. If she hadn't heard Saud ... If Raoul had not returned ...

Over and over her mind kept playing back to her the sound of the snake's soft movements, her throat gagging with fear, until sleep at last claimed her in a stifling, thick embrace.

CHAPTER EIGHT

NIGHTMARES tormented her uneasy sleep—muddled images of the dining-room at the Dorchester, men with guns which turned into writhing snakes—and Claire woke up, her heart pounding, her body bathed in perspiration, a sudden movement in the shadows by the door making her tense and call out in fear, 'Who's there?'

'Only me.' Raoul detached himself from the shadows. 'I'm sorry if I startled you, but you were crying out in your sleep.'

Shivering, Claire admitted huskily, 'Every time I close my eyes I keep hearing that snake, I keep remembering what happened in London . . .' She shuddered and then tensed in disbelief as Raoul walked towards her bed, casually pulling back the bedclothes. 'What . . . what are you doing?'

For the first time she thought she saw a certain grim humour gleaming in the darkness of his eyes as he surveyed her pale features and tense expression.

'Since you cannot sleep properly because of your nightmares, and I cannot sleep for the sound of your fear, we might as well share what is left of the night together.' He was in bed beside her before Claire could protest, and treacherously an inner voice whispered that the warm weight of his body in bed beside her was comforting.

'Come.' When his arms came round her, pulling her

against his body, a different kind of fear raced through her veins, but the heat of his body pressed against hers was too compelling to resist. She wanted this, Claire admitted drowsily, she wanted this close union of their bodies, this comfort Raoul gave to her standing between her and her fears. But merely being held in his arms possessed its own form of torture and Claire was relieved when she felt sleep stealing over her, drowning out her desire to touch the taut male flesh against which her head was pillowed, to press soft kisses into the curve of his shoulder and feel his body harden with desire, in the same need she could feel stirring deep inside her.

When she woke again it was morning and Raoul was gone, the only evidence of his occupation of her bed the shallow indentation of his head in the pillow next to hers. She turned her face into it hungrily, breathing in the trace of his body scent, feeling her body tremble with longing. She heard Saud cry and was instantly jerked back into reality. They couldn't rule out the possibility that someone had discovered the truth, Raoul had said last night, and a sudden wave of nausea invaded her stomach.

That was the first time that fear had actually made her physically sick, she thought, minutes later, standing in her bathroom shaken and dazed by the intensity of her emotions.

Too lethargic from her broken night to want to make the long trek down to the beach, Claire told Zenaide that instead she would take Saud down to the main courtyard. 'It is quite sheltered down there but open enough for him to get some fresh air.' She knew that Zenaide was looking at her disapprovingly because she hadn't eaten her breakfast. Not even the delicious fresh fruit Zenaide had brought had been able to tempt her. Say nothing to anyone, Raoul had said, but the burden of keeping to herself what had happened was a heavy one. She couldn't suspect Zenaide, who was always so gentle and caring, nor Ali, but someone had been responsible for that snake ... there was someone in the palace they couldn't trust.

By the time she reached the courtyard her head was throbbing, her headache a legacy of her fear. Even Saud seemed to lack his normal vitality, crying to be picked up and cuddled rather than employing himself busily with his toys as he normally did. How on earth were they going to keep him safe?

Because she had been concerned about his diet, Claire had brought with them a large supply of baby food which she prepared herself. Poison was a favourite method of murder in the East, so she had read, and she shuddered thinking of someone administering it to her small charge. She must not think about it, she told herself, she must get a grip on her emotions. Already Saud seemed to have picked up on her nervy, fearful mood and was reacting to it. Perhaps Raoul would be able to discover something, to find out who was the culprit. From Zenaide, she knew that he had gone to the city; Ali had not driven him and Claire wondered if he had deliberately left the other man behind to watch over them.

She managed to eat some lunch—a little of the delicately flavoured rice Zenaide brought out to her, and some of the fresh fruit—but she was shudderingly reluctant to return to her rooms, especially with Raoul absent, even though common sense told her that whoever had put the snake in Saud's room was hardly likely to attempt the same thing twice. She could only hope that Raoul was right when he said that by saying nothing they might be able to lure the would-be assassin out into the open.

She was just on the point of returning inside when Zenaide came hurrying into the courtyard, her normally smooth forehead puckered into a frown.

'It is the Princess Nadia, Sitt,' she exclaimed anxiously. 'She has called to see you.'

'Princess Nadia?' Claire too frowned, wondering if she ought to recognise the name. Raoul had mentioned various members of his family to her following the Princess's visit, but had added that his family was so large and its members so numerous that it was pointless her trying to remember them all.

'She is second cousin to the Lord Raoul,' Zenaide told her, still looking anxious. 'Shall I tell her that you are resting?'

For some reason her maid did not like the Princess Nadia, Claire observed, but that was no reason for her to deny herself. She had no wish to offend any members of Raoul's family and so she smiled calmly and asked Zenaide to bring the Princess to the courtyard and to arrange for coffee and almond cakes to be served to them.

Not sure of the correct protocol, but guessing that the title 'Princess' meant that her visitor was of superior rank to herself, Claire stood up as she heard footsteps approaching the courtyard, frowning a little as she caught the impatient tap of very high heels. She had been expecting a woman of middle age, but the girl stalking arrogantly towards her, the *abba* which had been covering her from top to toe as she rounded the corner discarded, was only half a dozen years or so older than herself. With swift dismay, Claire registered the haughty, almost petulant expression, the clothes that shrieked Paris and clung seductively to her lusciously curved body. Eastern her visitor might be, but her hair and make-up quite definitely came from the most elegant Western salons. This was no shrinking flower of the desert, but a sophisticated woman of the world whose elegance did little to conceal a nature which Claire guessed to be both hard and avaricious.

Her deeply-glossed lips parted in the coolest of smiles as she approached, dismissing Zenaide with a few curt words.

'So, you are the woman Raoul married instead of me?' were her first devastating words, accompanied by a taunting smile and a narrowed assessing glance. 'You have not deceived yourself that he cares for you, or ever will, I hope?' she added insultingly, carrying on before Claire could draw breath to retaliate. 'And this must be the child who is the cause of your hurried marriage. The Sheikh, my uncle, is well-known to disapprove of mixed marriages. Indeed it was he who advised my father to forbid my marriage to Raoul.' She shrugged and added, 'I must confess I was glad. As a lover Raoul is superb, but as a husband...'

A shrug of elegantly clad shoulders mocked all Claire's previous conceptions of what Raoul's intended bride had been like.

'A husband is only to be tolerated when he remains in the background, and provided, of course, he is very rich. Raoul is far too possessive ever to make a complacent husband. The insecurity of his childhood, of course. I hear he was most reluctant to make an honest woman out of you, Miss . . . but, of course, Eastern men are renowned for the importance they place upon their eldest sons. How old is he?'

Desperately trying to hold on to her temper, Claire responded. So this was the woman Raoul was to have married, and who, if she was to interpret her remarks correctly, was still his lover. A wedding ring gleamed on her hand, so she must be married and, no doubt, used her marriage to protect her from any censure regarding her wanton behaviour. Muslims were very strict guardians of the morals of their women, but the Princess Nadia seemed to make her own rules.

Did Raoul love her? A quiver of jealousy burned through her at the thought, so tormenting her that she missed her unwelcome visitor's next question, and had to have it impatiently repeated, feeling very much like an ignorant schoolgirl being chastised by her teacher.

'Raoul, where did you meet him? It must have been when he was working at our Embassy in London. That was just after my marriage. My father asked the Sheikh to send him there. Poor Raoul, he took my marriage very badly. A hungry man will take whatever is available, is that not so, Claire? And a clever woman knows how to make the most of whatever opportunities come her way. A girl of your station in life cannot have had many. Raoul is very attractive as well as a very wealthy man, and you were clever enough to know exactly which bait to use to hook him. Is this his child? He does not look very much like him. I should have thought he would be much fairer skinned. Where was it you said you met?'

Saud had been pulling himself up on to his feet, and fell over, suddenly starting to cry. Claire went instinctively to pick him up, realising only as she straightened that Raoul had returned and was striding towards them. Nadia had her back to him, and Claire wondered if she had the courage to endure Raoul's reaction to the other girl's presence. But a little to her surprise, when Nadia did turn and see him, there was nothing but polite calmness in Raoul's eyes.

'Raoul . . .' Her arms went round him, the glossed lips pouting for his kiss. Claire averted her eyes, hating the fierce pangs of jealousy storming through her, fighting to appear calm and controlled.

'Princess Nadia was just asking if we met when you were working at your London Embassy, darling,' she managed to enunciate gaily. She wasn't sure where they were supposed to have met. Let Raoul do his own lying and his own explaining if Nadia should cross-question him afterwards. As they were lovers and apparently had been for many years, she would naturally expect to know about any other women in Raoul's life, although it was patently obvious that she did not consider Claire to be any sort of competition.

Her eyes dropped to Saud. He didn't look like Raoul, Nadia had said, and she had also commented on his olive skin. She started to worry at her lip, and was startled to hear Raoul saying curtly, 'It was the Paris Embassy at which I worked for a term, not the London . . .'

'Of course, Raoul,' Nadia was quick to intervene. 'That is what I said, Claire must have misunderstood me. It was just after I got married, wasn't it? I remember we visited you there when we were on our honeymoon. So where did you meet? You still haven't told me.'

'At a party given by a friend,' Raoul responded indifferently, surprising Claire by bending down to pick up Saud, who gurgled his pleasure, waving small fists excitedly in the air. Raoul must have been watching her, Claire thought dazedly, because there was nothing hesitant or awkward about the way he handled the child, and surely no one watching him would doubt that Saud was his. Claire had dressed him in cool cotton rompers, and the small chubby legs kicked enthusiastically. He had a small birthmark on his left thigh, and it caught Claire's attention as he wriggled in Raoul's arms. Nadia was looking at it too, and for a moment it seemed to Claire that the temperature in the warm, shaded courtyard suddenly dropped—enough to raise goosebumps on her exposed arms, and to bring back the terrors of the night.

Raoul noticed immediately. 'You are not well?' he asked sharply.

'I'm . . . I'm fine.' How could she explain the *frisson* of terror which had just shivered through her? There was no logical explanation, but she was glad when Nadia eventually exclaimed that it was time she left, waving aside the coffee and almond cakes Claire offered.

'Far too fattening,' she pronounced, and Claire was sure it was no accident that her painted fingertips moved seductively down the curve of her body, drawing Raoul's attention to every enticing curve. Compared with Nadia, she was a pale snowdrop put against the beauty of a deep red rose, and she suffered by the comparison.

When Nadia had gone, Raoul announced that he had brought some work back with him that he wanted to finish. Claire wanted to talk to him, to tell him that she suspected Nadia might have guessed that Saud wasn't their child, but perhaps Raoul himself had told Nadia the truth. But surely in that case she would not have raised the subject? It was too taxing a problem for Claire to unravel. Her broken night was beginning to catch up with her, and when Zenaide came in to ask what she wanted to have for dinner, she told the little maid that she wasn't hungry and that she had decided to have an early night.

Saud, fortunately, seemed to have recovered his normal good spirits, laughing and gurgling when Claire bathed him, splashing her with the warm water as he played with his ducks. She grew more and more attached to him with every day that passed and knew she would feel the wrench when she had to leave. If she felt like this about Saud, how would she feel if she had conceived Raoul's child? Could she bear to leave him with his father?

She hadn't conceived a child, she was sure she hadn't, Claire told herself fiercely. She didn't feel any different than she had before. But it was early days yet, an inner voice warned her, far too soon for her to know one way or the other. As she prepared for bed, she found herself praying again that there would be no child. Hadn't she already endured enough heartbreak?

She was just walking through from her bathroom to her bedroom when the outer door opened. Thinking it would be Zenaide she paused, but it was Raoul who walked in, causing her nerves to quiver in mute reaction.

'Zenaide tells me you are not eating.'

'I ate some lunch,' Claire corrected.

'You are not feeling well?'

She flushed as she realised he was probably thinking along the lines she herself had been earlier, and probably with as much regret. If he wanted any woman to bear his child, it must be Nadia. 'Just a reaction from last night, that is all . . .'

'I wanted to talk to you anyway. It occurred to me this afternoon that we ought to have some sort of story prepared. Nadia will not be the only person to question you about the past.' He frowned as though remembering something. 'I cannot think why you should have thought she said I was posted to our London Embassy. Nadia of all people should . . .'

'Know that it was to Paris you were sent when she was married?' Claire said tautly. 'She did say London, Raoul. A slip of the tongue, no doubt, but she lied when she told you I had made the mistake.'

'Lied?' His eyebrows rose. 'Why should she do that?'

'Perhaps because she resents my presence in your life,' Claire said with a calm she was far from feeling. 'Anyone who loves resents the presence of someone else in the life of their lover.'

'And does your lover resent my presence in yours?' he asked softly. 'He has not written to you recently. Have you written to him, Claire? Have you told him that you might be carrying my child? That we have been lovers?'

'No . . . no, I haven't told him anything,' Claire whispered truthfully. Raoul's softly-spoken words were conjuring up images she would far rather forget.

They had far too disturbing an effect on her composure. She glanced up and found him looking at her, probing the pale silk of her robe, reminding her how intimately he knew the curves that lay beneath. A hot languor spread through her veins; a tormenting desire to go up to him and press her body against his, wantonly offering herself to him, feeling him respond.

'And nor will you do so,' Raoul muttered arrogantly. 'You are my wife now, Claire, mine!'

She wasn't sure which of them moved first, she only knew that somehow she was in his arms, breathing in the warm male scent of him, feeling her pulses leap in exultation. She wasn't even going to think about what had brought him to her, what had sparked off his desire. He bent his head, and her lips parted eagerly, welcoming the probing invasion of his tongue, all her earlier insistence that there should be no intimacy between them forgotten as her body's craving overruled the fragile control of her mind. Her senses reeling wildly, she responded with all the banked down hunger inside her to the hungry dominance of his mouth, groaning with pleasure when his hand cupped her breast, stroking roughly over the thin satin barrier which separated his fingers from her flesh. Opening to him as eagerly as the furled petals of a flower to the sun, Claire drank in the touch and scent of him, sliding trembling fingers inside his robe, pressing her palms flat against the moist heat of his skin, thrilling to the hard possession of his mouth when her thumb rubbed lightly against the hard flesh of his nipple.

He dragged his mouth away from hers, plundering the soft scented skin of her throat, pushing aside her robe, copying the caressing movements her fingers had made against him. Shivering waves of pleasure crested and broke over her, her body the receptacle of sensations so acute that she thought she might break apart under the pleasure of them. Her tongue touched the strong column of his throat, feeling the muscles strain as he swallowed an involuntary moan of pleasure, urging her closer to him, his hands sliding down to her hips, and round to spread against the rounded curves of her buttocks, pressing her against him.

He was already hungrily aroused and the knowledge thrilled and excited her, her hips moving in instinctive enticement, her teeth nibbling delicately at the warm flesh between his neck and his shoulder. Raoul had taught her that love-making could be a sensual feast and now he was encouraging her to make for herself a banquet she knew no other man could ever rival. She wanted him as much, if not more, than he wanted her. She knew that male arousal was not as subtle as female, but her longing for him swept aside any rational doubts that might have made her think twice about what she was doing. When her body became impatient for his possession, she slipped out of her robe, pausing when she saw the look in Raoul's eyes. They glittered almost black in the dimly lit room and the hand he stretched out to her betrayed a fine tremble.

The drift of his fingers along the outline of her body, no more than a butterfly touch, was excruciatingly arousing, but some inner sense, some instinctive urge to respond to his rhythm held her still beneath it, her throat closing on a hungry moan of impatience as his fingertips brushed briefly over the curves of her breasts. Surely he could see what he was doing to her? How much she needed the solid contact of his body against hers? But again something prevented her from moving, from taking the few steps necessary to bring her against him.

'Claire.' He said her name thickly, picking her up and carrying her the short distance to the bed, removing his own robe before lying down beside her.

Her whole body trembled with an acute ache, her eyes closed so that he wouldn't see the depths of the hunger in them as he bent towards her. Disappointment shivered bitterly through her as she felt his brief kiss on her lips, his tongue stroking gently over them, when what she wanted was the fierce intensity she had felt in him earlier. His lips drifted gently across her skin, his tongue touching, arousing, and then withdrawing, all down the length of her body until she felt she might explode beneath his tormentingly tentative caresses. He paused when he reached her breasts, stroking their pointed aching tips briefly with his tongue, but when Claire reached up to him, her whole body surging beneath the caress, compelled by a fierce need to urge him to intensify the contact, his fingers locked round her wrists, forcing them slowly down to her sides, his tongue returning to stimulate her throbbing flesh, until Claire felt she could stand it no longer and her body began to move wantonly, perpetuating an ancient rhythm.

Almost instantly the gentleness left Raoul's touch, replaced by the hunger she had earlier yearned for, explosive in its unbridled demands; the searing touch of his mouth against her body wanted an intimacy that made her gasp and tense until he showed her how he wanted her to respond, and all her previously held ideas of what desire should be between a man and a woman were overturned in a storm of pleasure too intense to allow hesitancy or withdrawal.

When at last Raoul moved over her, her body quivered ecstatically in response, glorying in the surge of pleasure fusing between them as she arched to welcome his body into hers, her fingernails digging deep into the muscles of his sweat-slick back, the fierce sound of pleasure emitted from his throat echoing the elemental urgency she could feel soaring deep inside her.

All the delight in the universe seemed to be concentrated inside her; their bodies were no longer two separate entities, but one united whole, seeking and finding together the pleasure which was the nearest the human race could ever come to savouring eternity.

Afterwards she slept, deeply and dreamlessly, waking with the dawn, drowsy and satiated with satisfaction, her body as sleek and supple as a mountain cat's—until she turned her head and found that at some time during the night Raoul had left her.

CHAPTER NINE

It was Zenaide who told her that Raoul had gone to see his uncle, the Sheikh, and that he had left a message to say that he might be gone for several days. His uncle—or Nadia—Claire found herself wondering bitterly. He might have made love to her, but that didn't mean that he loved her. Her hand brushed against the flat curve of her stomach as she remembered the feeling of nausea she had experienced earlier, and her haunting fear that she might be carrying Raoul's child returned. Up until now she had managed to keep it at bay, reassuring herself that she could not possibly be pregnant, but now she wasn't so sure. And there was Saud to worry about as well. How could Raoul leave them now, after what had happened? And moreover leave them so that he could be with Nadia?

He had been gone three days before Claire could bring herself to admit that she was pregnant. Her persistent sickness and the growing fullness of her breasts made it impossible for her to hide from the truth, and she was sure that Zenaide too had guessed. On one front at least, though, she could not accuse Raoul.

She had noticed how closely Ali stuck to both Saud and herself, remaining in the vicinity even while they were in the courtyard, and Claire had become particularly careful about Saud's food, making sure that no one apart from herself had access to it.

The knowledge that she was to have Raoul's child pushed aside some of her overwhelming anxiety for Saud, her mind grappling with new problems and fears. How could she leave her child behind with Raoul when they were divorced? But how could she stay, even if Raoul were to permit her to do so? The ideal solution would be for her to leave before Raoul guessed that she was pregnant, but that would mean deserting Saud. Her problems seemed insoluble.

On the fourth day of Raoul's absence, Claire woke to the familiar nausea striking her as she tried to leave her bed. She had learned to move more gingerly, taking her time in dressing and leaving her breakfast until she was sure the sickness had subsided. She was down on the beach playing with Saud when she heard the sound of feet crunching along the path. Tension feathered across her nerves instantly, the fear of danger to Saud never far from her mind, but it was Raoul who was striding towards them across the sand.

It was only when she shaded her eyes from the sun to study him properly that Claire saw the glitter of anger darkening his eyes. Fear trembled through her as she wondered at the cause of it. Was he angry because they had made love? Had Zenaide perhaps said something to him that had made him realise she was pregnant? She hadn't intended to tell him yet, not until she was properly sure, but his first words drove all thoughts of the baby out of her mind.

'I am surprised to find you still here when your lover has been so anxious to contact you—even to the extent of contacting our London Embassy. Have you any idea how I felt,' he continued bitingly, 'when I was summoned from an important meeting to be told that someone had been making urgent enquiries about you?'

Someone? Fear struggled with incomprehension, until the truth dawned. Teddy must have been trying to contact her, or someone on his behalf. Had he had an accident, was he hurt? Anxiety took the place of fear, her emotions mirrored clearly in her eyes as she struggled to her feet.

'Teddy . . .' she began urgently, only to fall silent as Raoul said thickly:

'So it's true, you do love him, so much so that I merely have to mention his name and you are filled with concern for him.' A muscle beat spasmodically in his jaw. 'I wonder if he will still feel the same about you once he learns that you have given yourself to me . . . abandoned yourself to me would be a better description,' he added softly, 'because there was total abandonment in the way you offered yourself to me, wasn't there, Claire?'

What could she say? She was too worried about Teddy to bandy words with him. 'I must go back to the palace,' she mumbled unsteadily, her mouth feeling as though it were full of marbles. 'I must ring . . .

'Teddy?' Raoul interrupted viciously. 'By all means, if only to tell him that he will make no further attempts to get in touch with you while you are living here as my wife. Indeed, I shall be surprised if he wishes to once he knows the truth, and you *will* tell him Claire, otherwise I will do it for you.'

With that threat ringing in her ears, Claire followed him blindly back up the path to the palace. Saud was balanced easily in his arms, chattering away in his as yet indecipherable private language, unaware of the tense atmosphere existing between the two adults.

Mentally checking the time difference, Claire worked out that she ought to be able to get through to Teddy's school. She knew the number, but because of the language difficulties she was forced to ask Raoul to ask the operator for it. He had told her she could make the call from his study, and although she had never been in the room before, apart from noticing that it was furnished functionally rather than anything else, she paid little attention to her surroundings.

She had expected Raoul to leave once he had requested the number, but to her dismay after handing the receiver over to her, he lounged on one of the divans, watching her twisting the telephone wire in nervous fingers. Willing him to leave, Claire turned her back on him. Why was he staying? To make sure that she told her 'lover' about her marriage? Dear God, how was she going to be able to speak to Teddy properly with Raoul there?

At last, when she was on the point of giving up, someone answered the phone. A voice she dimly recognised as belonging to the headmaster's secretary spoke into it, and haltingly Claire asked for the headmaster, too pursued by fear for Teddy now to worry about what conclusions Raoul might draw.

'Ah, Miss Miles,' she heard the headmaster saying calmly. 'I'm so glad you've got in touch, and you must excuse me for not using your married name by the way, but I'm afraid I don't recall what it is . . .' He sounded so normal and calm that Claire felt a little of her tension easing away.

'Teddy,' she blurted out. 'Is he all right?

Someone's been trying to get in touch with me, I believe . . .'

'And you thought something was wrong? I'm so sorry my dear. Teddy is fine. No, we've been trying to contact you about the holidays. Teddy wrote to you, I believe . . .' He broke off and murmured something which Claire didn't catch, her mind recognising with appalled dismay that she had never replied to Teddy's last letter. 'Look, I'm getting him to come to the phone. I know you'll feel more reassured if you speak to him yourself. He badly wants to come out and see you,' the headmaster was continuing, 'and if it's at all possible, I should strongly recommend it.'

'But . . .'

She was about to protest when the receiver was put down and then she heard Teddy's familiar voice, weak tears of relief pouring down her cheeks at his, 'Hi, sis. You've remembered that I exist at last, have you? Look, can I come out and stay with you?'

'Look, Teddy, I don't think it's a good idea,' she managed to interrupt before he could continue. 'It's terribly difficult getting out here, and . . .' She broke off as the receiver was wrenched out of her hand.

Raoul was towering over her, his face almost white with rage. Before she could stop him, he muttered thickly, 'I told you what to tell him and what I'd do if you didn't . . .' And then as he raised the receiver to his ear, Claire distinctly heard Teddy's reedy voice exclaiming anxiously, 'Claire? Sis, are you still there?'

For a moment there was deadly silence, Raoul's eyes locking with hers. Claire trembled, knowing that he too had heard what Teddy said, and then he was speaking into the receiver, his voice oddly warm and reassuring as he intoned, 'Teddy? This is Raoul speaking, Claire's husband.'

Teddy must have said something, because there was a silence from Raoul's end, and then he was saying, 'Of course you can come out. Yes, that's right, there can be problems with flights, but we'll organise something. Yes, I'm looking forward to meeting you too . . .' He handed the receiver back to Claire. 'He wants to say goodbye to you.'

Numbly she spoke to Teddy, letting Raoul take the receiver from her when she had finished. Again a tense silence filled the room, and then Raoul said quietly, 'I think we'd better have a talk, don't you? No more lies, please, Claire,' he continued curtly when she would have spoken. 'You can't honestly expect me to believe that your supposed lover is a boy with his voice still unbroken, who calls you "sis". And I can't understand why you should have allowed the misconception in the first place.'

'Can't you?' Her voice was bitter. 'Perhaps it just seemed easier to let you go on thinking the worst about me. You'd already made your mind up . . .'

'And you didn't care enough to change it?'

Why should he sound so tired? Honesty compelled her to admit a little of the truth. 'It wasn't that. I just thought it would be easier . . . safer . . .' He looked at her and she forced herself to meet the look in his eyes.

'Safer? But it wasn't, was it, Claire? Do you honestly believe if I had known that, I would have . . .'

'Made love to me?' she ventured with a brave smile.

'Among other things. But what's done is done, and now I want the truth. All of it,' he added implacably.

Slowly she told him, taking a deep breath and

speaking in a low, husky voice.

'So the money was for Teddy's school fees?'

Claire hung her head. 'Yes . . . I would have helped without any sort of payment . . . I wanted to help because of Saud, but you were so cutting and unkind, and I'd been worrying for months about how I was going to afford to keep Teddy at school. It's almost his home to him, you see,' she added unconsciously, pleading with him to understand. 'Since we lost our parents he's been so insecure. I wanted to provide him with all that he would have had if our father hadn't died.'

'And what about you, Claire?' Raoul asked huskily when she finished. 'Was there no one who could have lifted the burden from your shoulders? You were what when you lost your parents? Seventeen? Eighteen?'

'Eighteen,' Claire admitted, swallowed hard, hardly able to believe that it was tenderness she heard in his voice. 'I . . . I was just about to start university, but of course that was impossible. My godmother helped as much as she could, but her second husband has a family of his own . . . She often gave me little treats . . . That visit to the Dorchester . . .'

'Foolish, selfless Claire,' Raoul murmured over her downbeat head, 'so ready to deny herself for the good of others. I will arrange for Teddy to come out and stay with us, and you need no longer concern yourself with his school fees.' His mouth tightened when he saw her expression. 'No, Claire. Teddy is now my responsibility.'

'But . . . but our marriage is only temporary,' Claire reminded him breathlessly, 'and he can't come out here. I had to tell him something,' she reminded him. 'I couldn't just disappear, so I went to the school and

I told him we were getting married, but ...' She licked her lips, suddenly frightened to admit to Raoul the lie she had told Teddy.

'But?' he prompted, frowning. 'You didn't tell him you were marrying a man of mixed race, is that what troubles you? The shock he will have when he sees me?'

'No!' Her protest was vehement and instantaneous. 'Of course not. Teddy wouldn't worry about a thing like that. No, I told him we were in love,' she admitted miserably. 'I didn't want him to worry, or suspect anything you see. There are several Arab boys at the school and if I had told him the truth, he might have let it slip and it could have endangered Saud ... Raoul, what's wrong,' she asked uneasily, watching the slow tide of dark colour creep up under his skin. 'I shouldn't have lied to him, I know, but it seemed the most sensible thing at the time. Are you ... very angry?'

'Only with myself,' he told her in a voice tight with pain. 'I was judging you by my own standards, Claire, and I find it humiliating to see how ignoble they are compared with yours. Of course Teddy must come out to see you, he has been anxious about you. You haven't replied to his letters.'

'I forgot,' Claire agreed, gnawing her lip gently, thinking how wonderful it would be to see her brother—and how impossible. Surely Raoul could see that?

'I'd love to see him,' she admitted, 'but we, I ... we can't, Raoul. He's not naïve. He's bound to realise that ... that ...'

'We aren't in love?' Raoul supplied for her. 'I think

you are worrying far too much. Children tend to accept things very much at face value. Once he knows that we are sharing a bedroom as do other married couples, I doubt he will give the matter another thought.'

'But we aren't,' Claire protested, 'I mean we don't share a room.

'No, but for the duration of his stay we shall do so. He can have my room and I shall share yours. No more protests, please, I assure you I shall not take advantage of the opportunities such intimacy will afford me. You are quite safe, Claire, you may accept my word on that.'

'And Saud?' Claire pressed. 'What . . .?'

'Leave that to me. I shall explain to him that Saud had been orphaned and that as I am his legal guardian he will be brought up by us. In fact, I have been thinking . . .' he glanced at her and smiled mockingly. 'Poor Claire, you have far too soft a heart, how are you going to deny the claims of your three "children" when the time comes to leave me and make your own life?'

'Three? But . . .' Her heart started to thud erratically, her hand going protectively to her stomach. Surely he didn't know?

'But we do not know yet that you have conceived my child?' Raoul taunted. 'Ah, Claire, I am hoping that you have.' He saw her thunderstruck, disbelieving expression and laughed. 'I want to keep you with me, Claire, and I will use every means I can to do so. You already love Saud, you can't deny it, and I have been thinking that even when it is safe to reveal his true identity he could have no safer or more secure home than one presided over by you. And your brother. He is how old? Twelve? He will need your care for many years yet, and not merely financially. And lastly there are our children, Claire. If you give them one tenth of the love you shower on Saud, they will indeed be fortunate . . .'

'I am surprised you want me as the mother of your children,' Claire said bitterly. 'You were betrothed to Nadia . . .'

'Who is of a different religion, and a world away from the warmly maternal creature that is you, Claire. Nadia leaves her sons to be brought up by others. I suffered from that myself and have always sworn that I would not allow a child of mine to be torn in the way that I was. That is why . . .' He broke off, and said instead, 'My uncle, the Sheikh, will approve. He has liked you from the start.'

'And because of that, and two children, you expect our marriage to continue? You don't even . . .'

'Even what?' he taunted. 'Want you? You know that is a lie, Claire. My body finds a pleasure in yours that heats my blood just to think of it, and you are not, I think, indifferent to me. It need not be a bad life. You will be financially secure always, you will have the love of your children, and the . . .'

'Desire of my husband?' Claire demanded bitterly. 'At least until he tires of me and turns back to his mistress. Oh, you need not deny it, Nadia told me that you were still lovers . . .'

'You are overwrought, and now is not the time for us to argue. Think about what I have said, Claire.'

'But are you sure you want it?' she murmured, almost beneath her breath. 'I thought you loathed me and that you couldn't wait for me to leave.'

He bent his head, his breath fanning her temple. 'If that were the case, would I have sought to ensure that you remain with me?' His hand pressed against her stomach as he brushed his mouth across her surprised lips, making his meaning quite clear. 'The first time I must admit I did not think of the possible consequences until it was too late. But the second . . .' He smiled teasingly, stunning her with the amusement she read in his eyes. 'Ah, the second time, I must confess that I hoped your womb might be receptive to my seed and that there might grow in it the child who would keep you here at my side.'

Later, alone in her room, Claire found herself dwelling on what he had said. There had been no mention of love, and her heart ached over that, but it was tempting to think he might be right when he said they could build a life together—Saud and their own children growing up, perhaps some tenuous emotion growing inside him for her once she was the mother of his sons . . . And wasn't it too late anyway to make any conscious choice? She was already carrying his child and she sensed that once he knew that he would never let her go. In his way he was to be admired, because he wasn't just denying her love, he was denying it to himself as well, and she sensed that, while Nadia would always hold his heart, as his wife he would accord her respect and outward support. But did she have the strength to settle for that? Did she have any choice?

After that the day slid lazily into one another, and although nothing more was said Claire knew she had made her decision, and that Raoul was aware of it. She still hadn't told him she thought she was carrying his child. They were due to collect Teddy from the airport at the end of the week and Claire intended to ask Raoul if it was possible for her to see a doctor at the same time.

He had not been able to discover who was responsible for the snake in Saud's cot, but no other attempts had been made to injure the little boy, and Claire was beginning to wonder if it had been merely an unfortunate incident after all.

The day before Teddy's flight was due, Raoul walked into her room unannounced, frowning heavily. 'I have to go away for a few days. It can't be helped, unfortunately,' he told her. 'There's been an uprising in one of the remote villages on the border. Someone's been stirring up political problems, casting religious doubts on the new education plans and I have to go and see if it can't be sorted out.'

'Is it ... is it the same people who tried to kill Saud?' Claire asked dry-mouthed, suddenly filled with dread.

'Possibly,' Raoul was cautious, deliberately casual, but Claire wasn't deceived, he was going into danger. She could so easily lose him!

'Raoul, you will be careful, won't you?' she begged, watching his frown deepen slightly as though he couldn't understand why she should be so concerned. Careful, she warned herself, another minute and he might guess the truth. If there was to be any dignity in the life she would share with him her love for him was something he must never suspect.

'I think I'm having your baby ...' she told him huskily, knowing with deep feminine intuition that this was her strongest weapon, her greatest chance of keeping him safe. For his child's sake he would take fewer risks, think more carefully. 'I was going to ask you if I could visit the doctor when we go to collect Teddy. It's early days yet, but ... but I'm nearly sure.' She couldn't stop herself from blushing as he looked at her and then came towards her, sitting on her bed, pulling her down on to his lap.

'So my prayer was answered,' he said softly. She was wearing a soft cotton dress that buttoned down the front and before she could stop him he was deftly unfastening the buttons. His palm felt warm against the bare skin of her stomach, still ridiculously flat. But the evidence was there in the fuller curves of her breasts as he unfastened her bra and exposed them to his warm gaze, his thumb gently probing her peaking nipple. 'My child.' There was something almost reverent in the way he breathed the words touching her breasts with tender lips; a curious fluttering stirred in her stomach as he pushed her back on the bed, his head lying gently against her stomach, his face turned into the warm skin. 'My child.' He said it again, his breath soft against her body, the tender way in which he kissed her bringing an aching lump to her throat and weak tears to her eyes.

He couldn't have been more adoring if he had actually loved her, and for the first time she realised how important his child was to him. She had glimpsed it with Saud, in the tender affection he had for the little boy, and she was overwhelmed by a feeling of humility, a great surge of love that compelled her to put her arms round him, cradling him against her body, feeling the awe and the vigorous sense of achievement in him because his body had proved itself so potently virile.

'You must take care when I am gone,' he murmured, slowly releasing her. 'I shall take you to see a doctor when I get back. And I shall come back, Claire,' he assured her. 'My child will not be brought up without its father or its mother. They will all be our children,' he added, as though he had looked into her mind and seen what she was thinking. 'Teddy, Saud and this . . .' he dropped a brief, hard kiss against her stomach, 'and this as yet unknown, growing within the protection of your body. We shall love and succour them all.'

When he left she was almost glowing with happiness. His things had been moved into her room, and he had reassured her yet again that he would not be absent for long. But her fragile bubble of happiness burst disastrously the following morning when Zenaide came in to say that Princess Nadia had arrived to drive her to the airport.

Raoul had said nothing about Nadia coming to drive her, but perhaps it was as well that this had happened, Claire decided miserably. At least it served as a reminder to her as to where his feelings really lay. He was glad now because she was carrying his child and would be a tender, caring father. But he would never love her as a woman—as he loved Nadia.

CHAPTER TEN

TRYING not to betray how dismayed she was that Nadia was driving her to the airport, Claire checked her appearance in her mirror. The pale buttermilk linen suit she had chosen looked chic and attractive, her skin betraying just the barest suggestion of a tan. Saud was going with her—Raoul had suggested that she take him—and as she went downstairs to meet Nadia Claire couldn't help wishing that Raoul was there to go with them instead.

Nadia, as before, was expensively and elegantly dressed, her eyebrows rising slightly as she ganced at Claire's suit.

'Chanel?' she questioned unhesitatingly. 'But then Raoul always was very proud and he would scarcely want it to be said that he could not afford to keep his wife decently clothed. He said to tell you that he might be delayed, by the way,' she threw casually over her shoulder as she led the way to the car, and Claire had to bite down on the exclamation of dismay which sprang to her lips. When had Nadia seen Raoul? He had promised to telephone her and she had stuck close to the palace all day waiting for his call. He could not find time to telephone his wife, but he did have time to talk to Nadia, or so it seemed.

The interior of Nadia's Mercedes was comfortably air-conditioned, the fine leather seats contoured to provide the utmost comfort, but Claire wasn't in the mood to appreciate the quality of the car's German engineering and attention to detail. Nadia said something to her chauffeur before closing the panel that separated the front of the car from the rear, leaning back in her seat and lighting a cigarette.

'So. You have a brother, Claire, and Raoul has discovered that he has another responsibility. It seems you have also been able to effect a reconciliation between Raoul and his father. You know I find that very hard to believe. Not even our uncle, the Sheikh, has been able to make Raoul overcome his bitterness towards his father—and it isn't even as though Raoul cares in the slightest about you. Oh, come,' she drawled when Claire would have spoken, 'you and I both know the truth. Raoul might have turned to you in a moment of physical need . . .' she shrugged elegant shoulders, 'that is only to be expected, but he does not love you Claire.

They had been driving towards the city and Claire frowned as they suddenly veered off the main road, heading for the desert. 'A short cut,' Nadia drawled languidly, noticing her reaction. 'It will help us to avoid the congestion of the souk. Have you been there yet, Claire? Most Europeans find it interesting. Has Raoul told you that had he been born of the Sheikh's brother and not his sister our marriage would have been permitted? That would have meant that in time Raoul would have succeeded the Sheikh.' She spoke almost absently and yet Claire had the feeling that something important was hidden in her words. 'In the East, the only way for a woman to wield power is through her husband. My husband is third in line to the throne. He was fifth in line until my cousin was killed, a most unfortunate accident, and then his baby son too was murdered, in London as it happened. He would have been about the age of your Saud. Indeed, I believe there is also a certain physical resemblance, although I must admit that I only saw the child twice. But then, of course, they are related. Why, Claire,' she commented, watching her, 'you have gone quite pale. Are you quite well?'

'It is nothing,' Claire assured her, driven by some impulse to inflict her own wounds by adding casually, 'The early weeks of pregnancy can sometimes be uncomfortable. You have two children of your own Raoul tells me, so you will understand . . .'

'You are carrying Raoul's child?'

Something had gone wrong, because there was triumphant delight in the dark brown eyes instead of the angry jealousy Claire had expected to see, and when she glanced out of the window Claire was disturbed to see that they were surrounded by desert, with the city nowhere in sight.

She glanced at her watch, frowning as she realised the time.

'My brother's flight——' she began urgently.

'Unfortunately you will not be there to meet it,' Nadia interrupted with ill-concealed venom. 'You are far too trusting, Claire, and have played right into our hands. Hasim was right to guess that you would be our most powerful weapon. You and Saud, who we both know to be the son of my cousin, my dead cousin,' she repeated, 'and not Raoul. Oh yes, it was a clever move, and for a time you had us fooled. We truly believed that Saud had perished as he had been intended to, but Hasim was suspicious about this marriage between you and Raoul, and about the child you were supposed to have borne him. Raoul is a clever man, but not clever enough. He forgot about this.' She touched the birthmark on Saud's leg mockingly. 'This is something Saud inherited from his mother. She was my half-sister.' Her mouth curled in mocking contempt. 'She was also my father's favourite. I was too much a rebel, too greedy for power and riches—like Hasim. Has Raoul told you nothing of Hasim, my brother?' she added. 'It was Hasim who urged my father to forbid the marriage between us. Raoul, like the Sheikh, is far too philanthropic. If it were left to them all the wealth we derive from our oil would be wasted on coaxing the desert to flower, on educating ignorant tribes people, but they will not be allowed to do so. Now that we have Saud we can force the Sheikh to abdicate and Hasim will take his place on the throne. We have turned too much to the West in recent years, but once Hasim is in power things will be different.'

Nadia's brother was the leader of the rival faction? Did Raoul know of this?

'Raoul, of course, suspects nothing of this. No one does,' Nadia continued, almost as though she had guessed Claire's thoughts. 'Hasim has been at great pains to remain in the background, but soon the day will come when he can take his rightful place as leader of our country, and you have helped us, Claire. With Saud in our hands my uncle will refuse us nothing, and I am sure that Raoul will also pay us well for the return of his wife, especially as she is carrying his child.'

'I thought you loved him.' The words escaped stiff lips as Claire tried to come to terms with what Nadia had told her.

'Loved him? A man who considered his pride more important than me? He could have changed his religion as my father directed but he refused, and humiliated me with his refusal, and I swore then I would be revenged upon him. Of course, he does not know how I feel. It is very easy for a woman to conceal her true feelings from a man, isn't it, Claire? I believe you love him, don't you?'

Averting her profile, Claire stared out of the window. Ahead of them she could see a fringe of palm trees against the horizon and bleakly remembered the oasis she had visited with the Princess. As they travelled along the straight road, the palm trees grew larger and Claire saw that they were indeed heading towards a small oasis, although whether it was the same one she had visited earlier she could not tell. Half a dozen black tents stared blindly at them as the Mercedes swept past in a cloud of dust. Nadia laughed tauntingly as she saw her expression. 'Ah no, I'm afraid there will be no opportunity for escape nor for rescue . . .'

'But Raoul will know the truth, he will know that I left for the airport with you.'

'By that time it will not matter. Once we let the Sheikh know we have Saud, we shall no longer need to preserve any secrecy.'

Although she talked glibly about ransoming her, Claire suspected that neither she nor Saud would be allowed to live, and as she looked down at the small boy asleep beside her Claire thought wretchedly how she had let him down—and not just him but Raoul as well. Her hand fluttered towards her stomach, the gesture arrested by Nadia's mocking laughter. 'Poor Raoul, he will be beside himself with concern when he learns what has happened, won't he, Claire? Not concern for you, of course, but for the child you carry. You can only be in the very early stages of pregnancy, an acutely vulnerable time . . .'

She wasn't saying anything that hadn't already raced through her own mind, and Claire turned her face back to the window, pushing down the hood of her burnous as she stared through the tinted glass with burning hot eyes. She wouldn't give Nadia that satisfaction. A cloud of dust on the horizon caught her attention, and Nadia grimaced as the Mercedes swiftly overtook a small cavalcade.

'Badu! The Sheikh and Raoul seek to educate them—when Hasim is in power money will not be wasted on such folly.'

'If your brother does turn towards Russia, do you honestly suppose you will be allowed to retain your wealth?' Claire asked quietly. 'A communist country would never . . .'

'I shall not stay here.' Anger flashed in the dark eyes. 'Hasim has promised that when this is over I can live wherever I wish. The world shall be my oyster, Claire.'

'And your brother, does he honestly believe he will be able to retain control of the country?'

'Hasim is clever. He has the support of a certain religious faction which is against our present progress. Omarah is too far away from Russia to be strictly controlled, and we have the wealth to protect ourselves.'

So Hasim would use Russian aid to gain control of the country and then once he had he would betray his former allies? Somehow Claire did not think he would be allowed to get away with such treachery.

It was growing dusk when eventually the Mercedes came to a stop at a small oasis. A cluster of tents crouched by the waterside. 'Out,' Nadia commanded, thrusting open the door, and wrinkling her nose fastidiously as they were enveloped in a cloud of sand. A small, squat man, heavily robed, approached the car.

'Well, brother dear, I have brought them to you as I promised,' Nadia called out gaily, 'and it is even better than we hoped. She is carrying Raoul's child.' She cast a taunting look over her shoulder at Claire. 'So we shall have to be extra caring of her welfare. Any news from the others?'

The man she had addressed as her brother switched into harsh Arabic, and both of them ignored Claire as she stood swaying in the darkness, overcome by heat and exhaustion, Saud a heavy weight in her arms. They were miles from anywhere and even as the thought of escape occurred to her, she was forced to admit that there was nowhere for her to escape to.

'You will be pleased to know that your husband is busy trying to vanquish the rebels,' Nadia taunted her, reverting once more to English. 'But my brother's men are skilled guerrillas and it will be some days yet before Raoul is able to return. By that time we will already have been in touch with the Sheikh.'

Before Claire could stop her, she picked Saud from her arms, showing him to her brother, pointing out the tiny betraying birthmark.

'We lost three valuable people in London. As well as paying for you, Raoul will have to make reparation for them. I hope he values his child-to-be highly, Claire, for if he does not . . .' She laughed when she saw Claire's expression and tormented, 'Oh you need not worry, we shall not hurt you, you will simply be set free . . . The desert has its own methods of punishing intruders.'

She was taken to a tent, far less luxurious than the one she remembered from before, and a surly girl brought food and water. Saud was fretful and remembering how cold desert nights could be, Claire wished she had something to wrap round him to keep him warm.

Although she had been sure that she would never sleep, she did so, so heavily that it occurred to her when she woke, cramped and cold just before dawn, that her food must have been drugged. Her main fear that Saud would be taken from her had not been fulfilled. As their chances of escape were nil, it was probably easier to allow her to continue looking after him, Claire decided, trying to coax him to drink a little of the water she had been brought by the same surly girl who had served them the night before.

She could hear sounds of activity from outside, and then the flap of the tent was thrust aside, and Nadia strolled in. 'Farewell, Claire,' she drawled. 'From now on Hasim will take care of you. I am returning to the city—to see how the Sheikh reacts to our demands. I doubt we shall meet again . . .' She was deliberately trying to frighten her, Claire knew, but she refused to give in to the insidious tug of fear spreading swiftly through her veins.

'You will never be able to get away with this,' she retorted with more assurance than she could feel.

'You think not? Who is there to stop us? Raoul will never discover where you are. Never!'

Claire knew that she was probably quite right. After the tent flap was dropped in place behind Nadia, she heard the Mercedes purring away and then silence, punctuated only by brief outbursts of Arabic. Apart from the same girl who had brought her food earlier Claire saw no one all day. She tried to keep her spirits up by playing with Saud and by forcing herself to take some simple exercise—walking up and down her tent—but the relentless tide of fear she was constantly trying to hold at bay wouldn't relinquish its cruel grip.

Another night passed, another dawn was heralded by the now familiar sounds of the camp, then disturbed when Claire heard the sound of a vehicle arriving and a staccato burst of conversation. Had the Sheikh responded to their threats already? She was being foolish to hope, Claire berated herself, Hasim would never allow them to go free. While Saud lived there would always be another contender to the throne. Instinctively her arms fastened tightly round the little boy as she heard impatient footsteps approaching the tent.

They were taken outside and forced to sit beside the oasis as Claire witnessed tents being taken down and placed in sturdy Land-Rovers, and heard shouted, muddled instructions on the cool morning air. As the sun gradually rose, all signs of occupation of the oasis were swept away. They were obviously going to move on, but why? Had the Sheikh somehow discovered where they were? Hope flamed in Claire's heart, only to be doused when Hasim approached her. He was flanked by two men, both carrying rifles, and Claire stiffened automatically, remembering the scene in the breakfast-room of the Dorchester.

'Thanks to the ingenuity of your husband, we are forced to move on to a more secure place. Oh no, you are not to come with us,' he murmured, when Claire moved towards the nearest Land-Rover. His eyes rested on her body and he shifted uncomfortably from one foot to the other. 'Is it true that you are carrying his child?'

When Claire nodded her head, too weary and terrified to lie, he grimaced. 'You will not survive to bear it, I fear, but as any man who takes the life of a woman with child is thrice cursed by Allah, I cannot do as Nadia would no doubt insist and use these,' he indicated the guns carried by his men, 'to bring your life to an end. You have two choices. Either you leave the oasis now, taking the child Saud with you; or you remain here, where you might survive until you are found, but we shall kill the child before we leave.'

It was no choice at all and he knew it, Claire thought bitterly. How could she even contemplate saving her own life at the cost of Saud's? Once they walked into the desert they might as well be dead, she knew that, but she also knew that she would not even think of trying to save herself by sacrificing Saud.

'I choose the desert,' she said proudly, lifting her head to meet the cold dark eyes, 'and I give thanks to Allah that he gives special care to women in my condition.'

'Personally I care nothing for these old superstitions,' Hasim told her callously, 'but my men have learned of your condition and would doubtless react adversely if I killed you or instructed them to do so, and until I have taken my uncle's place I shall need their support. Now . . . walk . . .'

Refusing to give in to the urge to look behind her, Claire did as he instructed. With every step she half expected to hear the whine of bullets behind her, but it seemed Hasim had spoken the truth when he had said that his men would not kill her.

'Walk and keep on walking for two hours,' he called after her. 'If you attempt to return to the oasis before that time is up, Saud will be killed.'

And if she kept walking for two hours, the oasis would be lost from her sight, Claire thought bitterly. It had taken six hours for them to reach the oasis—in a car—and although she was following the road, she knew quite well that she would die, of thirst and heat, before she could reach safety. Feverishly she tried to think. Perhaps if she only walked at night. It was colder then . . . but how long could she exist without water? How long could Saud exist? Already he was a heavy burden for her to carry, and already the horizon was wavering in front of her. She stopped and turned. Hasim was standing watching her, rifle slung casually over his arm. No, her only option was to go on . . . and on . . . her mind thought drearily as two hours melted into three and she had no clear idea of where she was going, the road a dark ribbon where it wasn't obliterated by sand.

Saud was awake, demanding to be put down. Surely it wouldn't hurt her to stop for a brief rest? Three hours. Hasim would have left the oasis by now. She could turn back, but as she did so, Claire was attacked by swirling dizziness. She forced herself to walk back, counting her footsteps, forcing herself to concentrate, unaware until she found herself ankle-deep in sand that she had somehow strayed off the road. It was a physical effort to keep her eyes open, her skin burned, her body flinched from the scorch of the sun. She had to sit down and rest . . . and it didn't matter really if she did. She had plenty of time . . . all the time in the world . . .

Someone was speaking, dimly Claire recognised the harsh Arabic sounds. She forced her eyes to open, her lids feeling like heavy weights. Someone was leaning over her, a man robed and wearing a head-dress, his features concealed by the thickness of his beard. Vaguely she was aware of deep-set dark eyes, and the curved arrogant blade of his nose, and then everything started to slip away from her. There was something important she had to say, but she couldn't remember what it was. She roused herself again and this time she was aware of subdued, high-pitched chatter that she remembered from somewhere. She must have made a sound because the chatter stopped. Someone was offering her water, and she gulped at it greedily, suddenly remembering.

'Saud . . . Saud . . .' she cried weakly, but there was only silence, and the memory of burning hot sands and clear cloudless skies from which a relentless sun burned down.

Claire opened her eyes. She felt as though she had been asleep for a very long time. Her body felt unfamiliar, heavy and tender, her eyes gritty.

'Lord Raoul, the Sitt is awake.'

Zenaide. Claire recognised her voice, and yes, this was her room in the palace. Had it all just been a dream, then, that searing heat, that sense of fear, that walk with Saud . . . Saud . . . She struggled to sit up and was instantly restrained by Raoul's arm.

'Saud,' she protested weakly.

'He is fine.' She heard Raoul bite off an expletive and then turn to Zenaide. 'He is perfectly well, Claire, Zenaide will bring him to you. There is someone else waiting to see you, too.' He was watching her closely, and Claire wished she could remember properly. Something eluded her, tugging at the edges of her memory, but she could not summon it up. 'It's Teddy,' Raoul pressed. 'Your brother. Remember, you were to meet him at the airport.'

The airport. Nadia! She must have said her name out loud because Raoul's face tightened.

'That is enough for now, Raoul.' Another voice spoke close by her, and a man moved from the shadows. 'She is still tired and must be allowed to recover. Without you beside her, my friend,' the unfamiliar voice continued, although it seemed to Claire that it held compassion. 'There is nothing more you can do. Punishing yourself will achieve nothing.'

Punishing himself? Why should Raoul do that? Because of Nadia? Because the woman he loved had helped to try to murder Saud? Did he know about that? Thoughts too exhausting to be sustained flooded through her tired mind, and then something else surfaced.

'Raoul.' She clutched at his arm. 'My baby . . .' A

look of bitter sadness filled his eyes, and her own clouded with tears. 'Raoul, my baby . . .'

'Your baby is quite safe.' It was the other man who spoke, smiling down at her, his fingers feeling for the pulse in her wrist with a professionalism that put her fears to rest. 'But that is more than can be said for you. You must sleep now if you are to recover your full strength. Later you can talk.'

'Saud,' she pleaded, 'I must see Saud . . .' She saw Zenaide coming into the room, Saud in her arms, and she expelled her breath on a thankful sigh, gladly submitting to the sleep stealing slowly through her veins.

When she woke again Teddy was sitting on the end of her bed, watching her. 'Good. Dr Naud said you would soon be awake. I would have to miss all the excitement,' Teddy continued, obviously aggrieved. 'Boy, when I tell them about it at school. It must have been really ace . . . to be kidnapped and then . . .'

'I am sure your sister found her experience anything but "ace", Teddy,' Raoul's voice said drily from the door. Teddy scrambled off the bed as Raoul approached.

'But it was ace how the Badu found her and looked after her, wasn't it?' he probed. 'Boy just imagine being able to track like that . . . and recognising her too when Nadia drove her past the oasis. "Lady of the golden hair" they call you,' he told a bemused Claire, grinning a little. 'Just think if they hadn't seen you and sent word to Raoul . . .'

'That's enough, Teddy.' Raoul's calm firm voice cut through Teddy's excitement. 'Ali has prepared your dinner.'

'But what about you?'

'I will eat up here with your sister.' Teddy looked ready to protest, but something in Raoul's expression must have changed his mind because he went off without another word. 'Oh for the recuperative powers of the young,' Raoul said lightly when he had gone. 'When we first learned that you were missing he was inconsolable.'

'You know everything?' Claire whispered. 'By 'everything' she meant Nadia's treachery, and Raoul nodded.

'Yes, and I cannot see how we could have been so blind. In so many ways it was obvious, but because Hasim remained out of the country for long periods we never thought to connect him with the left-wing faction in the country, even though he is the Sheikh's heir after Saud.'

'What happened?' Claire pressed. 'I . . .'

'Let me tell you from the beginning.' Raoul perched himself on the end of her bed, and Claire looked away from him, wishing he would come closer, take her in his arms perhaps.

'As Teddy has just said, you were recognised as Nadia drove you through the Badu encampment—that was her main mistake. Nadia and her family are well known for their contempt of the Badu, and Ali ben Durai's curiosity was aroused enough for him to send some of his men out after you. He knew, in the way that the Badu always seem to know what is going on, that your brother was due to arrive and that you were to meet his plane. He also knew that I was away, but when his suspicions were confirmed, he sent messages both to me and to the Sheikh telling us that he feared you had been taken captive. One of the men on the Sheikh's staff here at the palace was a spy—the same one who placed the snake in Saud's cot, I suspect—and he managed to send Hasim a warning that we were on our way.'

'So that was why he broke camp.' Claire shivered. 'They were going to kill us, but because I was carrying your child . . .'

'I know it all.' Raoul looked grim, and Claire wondered if he was thinking about Nadia. 'Hasim was most impressed with your courage, Claire. You risked your own life for Saud, choosing almost certain death rather than safety. If you had opted to remain at the oasis you would at least have had water and would have been found in due time, even if we had not known where to look, but instead you braved the desert.'

'They meant to shoot Saud,' Claire said unsteadily. 'I knew that we probably wouldn't survive the desert, but I couldn't . . . couldn't . . .' Tears started to burn her eyes and she turned away, too soon to see the movement Raoul made towards her. As she turned from him as though in rejection his arm dropped to his side, his expression suddenly grave.

'You are tired and the doctor has ordered that you must rest. When the tribesmen found you they feared it was already too late. They sent word to me and took you back with them to their camp.'

'And you brought me back here,' Claire finished for him. Now that Saud was safe, would he still want her to stay? Would he still want them to live together as a family, or had he changed his mind? There was something different about him, she knew that.

'My father sends his love,' Raoul told her as he

stood up, watching her eyes widen as he spoke the words. 'When he worked here—before he met my mother—he made a survey of the desert. I telephoned him to check that the oasis was where the Badu tribesmen had described. We couldn't afford to waste any time.' He sighed, pushing his fingers into the thick darkness of his hair, and suddenly looked tired and defeated. 'When I was a child, my grandfather constantly told me how my father had deserted my mother, how he had taken her money and left her, insisting that I was to be brought up as a Christian, and I hated and resented him. But the story he told me differs from that of my grandfather. Perhaps the truth lies somewhere in between, I don't know, but suddenly it no longer seems so important. What is past is past, and I too now know what it is to feel bitter corroding regret for my own actions.'

He turned, leaving her, and Claire's heart ached. Was he talking about Nadia? Wishing he had not been too proud to change his religion; thinking that if he had, his love might have saved her from becoming involved in Hasim's machinations?

By the end of the week the doctor was pleased enough with her progress to allow her to get up and spend the pleasant hours of the morning in the main courtyard, Teddy and Saud keeping her company. When she mentioned to Zenaide one day that more than anything else she would like to go down to the beach, Raoul appeared as though by magic and insisted on carrying her down to the soft fine sand. He swam in the azure sea with Teddy. She watched him coming out of the water, his body sleek and bronzed, her memory replaying disturbing scenes inside her head as she stared helplessly at him, sick and aching for the touch of his skin against hers.

Raoul mistook the reason for her pallor and cursed himself for allowing her to get overtired. There was no point in her objecting when he insisted on taking her back to the palace. He was treating her as though she were made of Dresden china, and sometimes she thought she couldn't bear it. What had happened to the man who had told her so arrogantly that he wanted her, that they would build a good life together? The strangeness she had sensed in him grew, and towards the end of Teddy's holiday she learned why.

He sought her out in the courtyard one morning when she was playing with Saud. Pregnancy had brought a soft glow to her skin, a warm ripeness of which she was unaware as she laughed at Saud's attempts to walk.

'I have booked Teddy's return flight,' Raoul told her, bending dexterously to catch Saud as he fell. His face was turned away from her, his voice perfectly even as he said, 'If you wish, you can be on that flight, Claire. No, say nothing now,' he urged when she wanted to protest. 'Think about it and then tell me what you wish to do. I think perhaps it would be for the best if you were to go.'

He left then, while she was still trying to come to grips with the enormous pain. Because of her weakness after her ordeal, Raoul had not shared her room as they had planned, but had slept in another on a separate floor. He was so distant and aloof these days that there seemed no way Claire could reach him. Why had he changed his mind about continuing their marriage?

Because of Nadia? But what about their child?

Anxiety and pain made it impossible for her to eat, and telling Zenaide that she no longer needed her Claire made up her mind what she must do. Raoul seemed to be at pains to avoid seeing her alone, but how could she talk to him—how could she make him see that he owed it to their child to allow her to stay? She wasn't going to give in easily. Now, when she was faced with the reality of leaving him, Claire knew that she would fight to be allowed to stay.

She entered his room without knocking and found it empty. For a moment she thought he must still be working downstairs, but then she heard the sound of running water from his bathroom and she curled up on the divan beneath the window, knowing that if she remained standing she wouldn't be able to stop herself from pacing nervously about the room.

When he walked in from the bathroom he didn't see her at first. His hair was damp from his shower, his body gleaming beneath the soft Moorish lamps whose diffused light Claire had come to love during her stay. And then as though some sixth sense alerted him to her presence he wheeled round, his body tensing almost as if in expectation of a blow.

'Raoul, I had to see you,' Claire told him before he could speak, 'and this seemed the only way. Do you ... do you really want me to go back to England with Teddy?' she asked him before her courage could desert her.

'It seems the wisest course.' He wasn't looking at her, reaching instead for the towel he had dropped on the bed. Against the brief one he had fastened round his hips, his body glowed the colour of warm honey, the muscles in his back as fluid as ripples of water on the surface of the gulf as he started to dry himself.

'But our child,' protested, refusing to heed the dismissal in his voice. 'You said . . .'

'Forget what I said.' Suddenly his voice was harsh, his eyes darkening to jade as he turned to her. 'Do you *know* how close you came to losing your life?' He looked so bitter, so caught up in whatever emotion it was that brought the deep-carved lines bracketing his mouth and the emptiness to his eyes, that for a moment Claire was lost for words.

'But I didn't lose it,' she reminded him. 'I'm safe and so is Saud. Oh Raoul, do you honestly want your son to be brought up as a stranger to you, as you were to your father?'

For a second Claire thought her impassioned speech had burst through the wall he had built around himself, but then he smiled with a return of the old mockery she remembered. 'My son? You are so sure then that this child you carry will be a boy?'

'Son—daughter—both have a right to your love, your presence in their lives,' Claire told him, wondering if he was aware of how much she was gambling, of how fast her heart was racing.

'You make a very convincing advocate, Claire,' she heard him say at last. His voice changed suddenly, full of bitter yearning as he added roughly, 'Do you really think you need to persuade me that I want both you and my child here with me? Do you have any conception of how hard it is for me even to contemplate letting you go? And that is even when I take into consideration how close you came to death, and all through my fault. If I had seen through Nadia earlier . . .'

'How could you when you loved her so much?' Claire said softly, wanting to take the look of burning pain from his eyes.

'Loved her?' He stared at her. 'Loved Nadia? What game are you playing now, Claire?' he demanded curtly. 'Nadia was once to have been my wife and would have been had I changed my religion. But I was too proud to do so, and for a while I told myself I was bitter because my religion set us apart, blaming my father because he had insisted that I was brought up as a Christian. But I tell you this, Claire, were religion all that stood between me and gaining your love I would gladly change it ten thousand times over. My father was right when he warned me against pride,' he continued, before Claire could draw breath. 'I thought I could compel you to remain here with me. I knew, you see, that you could never bring yourself to desert your child, not when you could hardly bear to be parted from Saud, and . . .'

'And yet now you want me to leave,' Claire stormed at him. 'You say you want my love and yet you want to send me away; and I don't even know why you should want it, you have never once . . .' She broke off in confusion when she saw the way he was looking at her. Never before had she seen such a look of burning intensity in his eyes, a look that was a complex blend of tenderness and intense desire.

'Never once have I what?' he asked her. 'Told you that I love you?' Self-mockery darkened the already deep colour of his eyes. 'I have not perhaps mouthed the words, but there are other ways, Claire, ways that rely on a touch . . . a look. Many, many times I have looked at you with all the love I feel for you, but you have never noticed it, and every time I touch you it is the touch of a man deeply in love. Why else do you think I want to send you away? I cannot expect you to stay here after what happened. No matter how much I personally want and need you by my side. Even if your love for me was as great as mine for you. Are you so blind, Claire?' he asked whimsically. 'Do you truly believe, knowing what you do about my past, that I would even contemplate you bearing my child if I had not fallen so deeply in love with that merely being in the same room, breathing the same air, is the most acute pain. I think I loved you from the very first, although I managed to hide my feelings even from myself. I told myself that you were greedy, avaricious; that you could not be the warm, loving person you seemed, that your love for Saud must be faked, that your responsiveness in my arms was only hunger . . .'

'If it was, then it is a hunger that only you can satisfy,' Claire managed to get out tremulously, her legs threatening to collapse beneath her as she stumbled towards the bed, swaying slightly so that Raoul was forced, almost against his will it seemed, to catch her in his arms.

'Oh, Raoul, please let me stay. Please tell me it's true and that you do love me.' The hesitant touch of her lips against the naked skin of his shoulder provoked a smothered groan of protest, his fingers biting deep into her slender arms.

'Do you really know what you are committing yourself to, Claire? Omarah is a very new country, and a great many years separate Saud from the maturity to rule it. Be warned that if you give yourself to me I will never be able to let you go. Already my nights are tortured by the memory of you in my arms, your body against mine. I thought we could build a life here together, until Nadia kidnapped you, and then I knew that no matter how much I loved you I could not risk your safety ever again.'

'Raoul, all that was at risk was my life,' Claire told him huskily, 'and without you in it, it is as arid and worthless as ... as the desert without water—a vast expanse of nothing.'

'As is mine without you,' Raoul muttered hoarsely, his strong body trembling beneath the teasing kisses she was placing against it. Behind her was the vastness of the Sheikh's bed, and Claire felt no guilt or restraint about allowing her body to slip down on to it, enticing Raoul's to follow, her arms outstretched to welcome him. The faint sigh he gave as he did so was half surrender, half impatiently stifled desire, telling her that there would be no departure from Omarah for her, not unless Raoul was at her side.

'Tell me again that you love me,' he demanded arrogantly as his lips brushed hers. 'I want to hear you say it.'

'Of course I love you,' Claire responded mischievously. 'Are you not the Lord Raoul, keeper of my heart, guardian of my virtue ... father of my child.'

'Worshipper of your body,' Raoul murmured as he feathered warm kisses across her skin. 'Lover of your heart.'

Beneath her the coverlet of silk shimmered in soft, rich blue waves, the evening breeze stirring hangings which had once graced the bed of the Sultan himself, but Claire was unaware of her surroundings. She had all that mattered safely encompassed within her arms, and the murmured words of love Raoul whispered in her ear were sweeter music by far than the soft desert breeze whispering through the silent courtyard outside.

Your FREE gift includes

Anne Mather—Born out of Love
Violet Winspear—Time of the Temptress
Charlotte Lamb—Man's World
Sally Wentworth—Say Hello to Yesterday

FREE Gift Certificate
and subscription reservation

Mail this coupon today!

Harlequin Reader Service

In the U.S.A.
2504 West Southern Ave.
Tempe, AZ 85282

In Canada
P.O. Box 2800, Postal Station A
5170 Yonge Street,
Willowdale, Ont. M2N 5T5

Please send me my 4 Harlequin Presents books free. Also, reserve a subscription to the 8 new Harlequin Presents novels published each month. Each month I will receive 8 new Presents novels at the low price of $1.75 each [*Total — $14.00 a month*]. There are no shipping and handling or any other hidden charges. I am free to cancel at any time, but even if I do, these first 4 books are still mine to keep absolutely FREE without any obligation.   **108 BPP CAEK**

NAME   (PLEASE PRINT)

ADDRESS   APT. NO.

CITY

STATE/PROV   ZIP/POSTAL CODE   P-SUB-3X

Offer expires September 30, 1984

If price changes are necessary you will be notified.